All of Me

Proofreading and editing by Laura M Walsh
Cover design by Kelly Pennington

ISBN: 978-0-578-91188-5

Dedication

To my husband, who is everything.

Chapter 1

Mia

I trudged up the 3 flights to my apartment loaded down with my groceries, work bag, and purse. I liked living on the top floor, I reminded myself for the hundredth time. I chose it on purpose. There were no neighbors walking around overhead and the view from my tiny balcony was worth the climb. My friend Meg was always telling me that stairs were good cardio and even better for toning your butt and legs. Who needed a gym when I had a 4th floor apartment to come home to every day?

Meg was forever trying to get me to join the gym she went to. I couldn't seem to convince her that it wasn't for me. The thought of working out in front of other people filled me with dread. I wasn't the most coordinated person and I was sure I'd find some way to embarrass myself. Unlike Meg, being the center of attention was the last thing I wanted. I had never been fond of the spotlight. I was trying to be less shy, more outgoing and sociable, but I doubted that would change dramatically anytime soon. Besides, no amount of working out or healthy eating was going to give me a great figure like Meg's. Growing up, my mom always said I was built like an adolescent boy – tall for my age, small boobs, no hips, and long legs. I'd topped out at 5'9" and had filled out a bit, but I was never going to have Meg's curves. On the rare occasions I let Meg talk me into going out to a club, all eyes were on her. That worked just fine for me.

I finally reached my floor. From the top of the steps I could see a package laying on the mat in front of my door. I had grabbed my mail from my mailbox on the ground floor on the way in, but this looked like it was way too large to fit in the small boxes we had. With my hands already more than full, I scooped it up the best I could and juggled everything while I unlocked and opened the door. Inside my apartment I stepped into my kitchen and dumped my whole load – purse, grocery bags, package, everything – on my small kitchen table.

What I really, really wanted to do was change out of my work clothes, microwave something for dinner, and relax on the couch with something mindless on Netflix. We were down a person at work and all the extra hours I was picking up were starting to get to me. The money was nice; the lack of energy to do anything else, not so much.

I quickly put away the groceries then went down the short hallway to my bedroom. I pulled the hair tie out of my hair and ran my hands through it. I had my mother's honey brown, lightly curly hair. I actually really liked my hair unlike so many women, but I almost always wore it up at work. It just tended to get in the way otherwise. I pulled on a pair of black leggings and pulled a baggy, washed-out blue sweatshirt over my head. On my way back through my kitchen I spotted my laptop on the breakfast bar separating the kitchen from the living room area and it reminded me that I had some bills to pay online. Mindless Netflix would have to wait a bit. I'd grab something quick for dinner and eat it while I sat on the couch with my laptop and paid bills.

As I thought about what to grab for dinner, I noticed the package I'd picked up off my door mat earlier. I'd forgotten all about it. I picked it up to see who had sent it and noticed that it wasn't even addressed to me. There were two apartments on each floor of my building separated in the middle by the center stairs and a large, open air landing. I was in 4A; the package was addressed to my neighbor across the landing in 4B. I didn't recall ever seeing my neighbor, but I thought the apartment had been empty for a while. My neighbor was apparently a man given the name on the package. I needed to take it over to him. I looked down at my comfy outfit and sighed. I wasn't exactly at my best to meet a neighbor for the first time, but whatever. I'd slip on my flip flops and take it over. I probably wouldn't even see him. I'd just leave it outside his door where the mail carrier had intended to leave it in the first place.

With the package in hand I opened the door, started to step out of my apartment, and saw the very man I had just been wondering about – my neighbor in 4B – unlocking his door. Damn it, I hadn't planned on actually seeing him, just putting the package in front of his door. He was tall, at least an inch or 2 over 6 feet, and from what I could see in t-shirt and jeans, he was amazingly fit. His back – his very large, muscular back – was to me, so he hadn't seen me yet. I thought about just slipping quietly back into my apartment, waiting until he closed his door, then taking the package over and leaving it on his doorstep like I had planned. But then it might sit there all night. What if it was stolen because I was too timid to speak to a neighbor for 10 seconds? Hadn't I resolved to put myself out there more?

Impatient with myself now, just as he was about to step through his door, I started toward him and spoke up.

"Mr. um…" Taking another quick look at his last name I realized it was a smudged and I couldn't make it out. Okay, first name it was then. "Um…Dante?"

I was completely unprepared for his reaction to me saying his name. I expected him to turn around, sure, but not to spin around with an intense glare and start toward me.

"What? What do you want?"

I stopped in my tracks and felt my breath, maybe even my heart, stop. "P…package."

I squeaked it out, barely able to speak past my shock at his aggression and his approach. I backed up a step and held out the package with a shaking hand. I couldn't keep my voice from shaking as badly as my hand.

"There's…..package…for you. Wrong…wrong address."

He stopped moving toward me, frowning first at what had to be the absolutely terrified look on my face and then down at the package in my hand. He took the package, still frowning, still not saying a word. As soon as the package left my hand, I began backing toward my door. There was no way I was turning my back on him. Just as I opened my door, my neighbor took a deep breath. I heard him say "Look…" as I shut my door behind me and locked both of my locks. He had his property back and my duty was done. Whatever he had to say, I didn't need to hear it.

Chapter 2

Dante

*W*ay to go, asshole. The first time I meet my closest neighbor and I scare the shit out of her. True, I'd been on edge lately and hearing my name out of the blue like that had surprised me. Still, I usually – like, always – had better control of myself. It had been an essential part of my game plan when I was still fighting. I didn't get all wired and crazy like some fighters. I didn't trash talk or show much emotion at all. I just took care of business. And won. A lot. Not every fight, but way more than most. It wasn't that I didn't feel anything during a fight – the adrenaline, the rage, the aggression were all there – I was just usually good at locking it down. Now that I was helping to train up-and-coming fighters at Dev's gym, I used that control to help fighters learn to stay focused, to center themselves and think clearly during a fight. Letting your emotions get the best of you during a fight was a sure way to lose. There were too many fighters who trained their bodies to be machines, fast and strong, but didn't bother to train their minds to be the same way.

Now with Pete constantly hammering on me about getting back in the ring, my well-known control was being severely tested. I'd told him to fuck off as nicely as possible – well, as nice as you can be when you're telling someone "Fuck no, go away" – but he wasn't listening. Pete was an okay guy, really. I'd known him forever and he was always just kind of...around. To be honest, he wasn't the brightest guy and there were people around who took advantage of that to get him mixed up in some shady shit. From the little I knew it was nothing major, nothing violent, just situations that probably weren't completely legal. I didn't know details and I stayed as far away from all of that as I could. Pete thought we were buddies, though, probably because I was one of the few people he knew who didn't treat him like crap. We didn't hang out together but he lived close by so I'd see him around sometimes. We'd talk for a minute or two and that was it. How he'd gotten this idea in his head that I should fight again was beyond me. It wasn't going to happen and he needed to drop it. He had even started hanging around outside the gym, catching me on my way home to bug me about it. The next time he asked – I was sure there would be a next time - I was going to have to find a way to shut it down for good. He was getting on my last nerve. Between Pete bugging the shit out of me and the news I'd gotten today that my baby sister had up and quit a great job with no explanation and now wasn't returning my calls, I was on edge. Add to that the long hours I was working and I was jumpy as hell.

As a result, I'd nearly taken the neighbor girl's head off for being a nice person and bringing my mail to me. I let out a breath. I was going to have to find a way to apologize. Although with the way she had looked at me, brown eyes wide and body shaking as she backed away, it wasn't going to be easy. I was still standing on the landing holding the package that had caused this whole thing. I could just go over, knock on her door, and apologize for being such an ass. I'd actually started to do just that when she essentially closed the door in my face. And quickly turned both of her locks. Yeah, I didn't think a knock on her door would go over well right now. I'd try later. Give her time to calm down and give myself time to think of something to say that didn't make me sound like an idiot.

～

Climbing the stairs to my apartment the next night I was still trying to think of what to say to the neighbor girl. The longer I let this go on, the worse her impression of me was going to be. As I reached the landing I saw the delivery guy from the Thai place on the corner standing in front of my neighbor's door. That gave me an idea. He saw me and gave me a nod. No doubt he recognized me from the many, many times he had delivered food to my apartment. What could I say? I liked Thai food and I wasn't much of a cook.

I spoke before he could knock on my neighbor's door. "Hey man, is that for 4A?"

His look said he thought the answer was more than obvious given that he was literally about to knock on the door. "Yeah, 4A."

"Here I'll pay for it. I need to talk with her, anyway."

The guy just looked at me, obviously unsure whether to hand over the food or not. I pulled out my wallet to show him I was for real.

"Look, I owe her a favor. I'll pay for her food, make sure she gets it, and she and I will be even." So I didn't really owe her a favor so much, though she had gotten my mail to me, but I did owe her an explanation and an apology. I knew I was basically tricking her into opening her door to me, but the way she'd looked at me yesterday this was probably the only way she would.

The guy shrugged, I paid him, and he took off. I stepped up to the door and knocked. If my neighbor looked through her peephole and saw it was me, not the delivery guy, she'd just have to decide how bad she wanted her dinner. I wasn't sure what I would do if she didn't open the door. I couldn't force her to talk to me. Luckily, I didn't need to figure that out, though. The door popped open and I saw the top of my neighbor's head as she looked down at the purse she was digging through.

"I'm going to have to do credit. I know I said cash on the phone, but.." she finally looked up and froze. I seemed to have that effect on her. And I wasn't even snarling at her this time, just standing there with her dinner order. Before she could unfreeze and slam the door in my face again, I quickly spoke up.

Chapter 3

Mia

"*I* need to apologize for yesterday."

It was my neighbor, Dante. Standing outside my door, holding what looked like my order from the Thai restaurant. And apologizing.

"Oh...um." Why could I not form sentences around this guy?

"Here." He held out the bag to me. "Your dinner."

"Where's Billy?"

"Who?" He sounded like he had no idea who I was talking about.

"The delivery guy."

"He was here. I took care of it. It's a peace offering." I thought... that was maybe...a smile on his face? Whatever it was, he looked less stormy and fierce than he had yesterday.

"Oh...well, thank you." I reached out and took the bag, careful not to brush his hand with mine. "You didn't have to do that, but thanks."

He nodded but didn't move away. Maybe I should be nervous after the way he had come at me the day before, especially since he was so close, but I found that I wasn't. Sure, I'd been a little rattled when I'd opened the door and he was standing there rather than Billy, but I was okay now. Actually he was the one who seemed nervous. He stood looking at the ground, running his left hand over his dark hair. It was buzzed really short, not my favorite look on a guy, but on him it worked. His skin had a warm olive tone that made me want to touch it to see if it was as warm and smooth as it looked. My impression from last night that he was tall and in amazing shape was confirmed. I had to look up at him and at my height that wasn't true of a lot of men. The dark blue t-shirt he wore molded nicely to his shoulders, arms and chest and he filled out his well-worn jeans really, really well. I found myself wishing he would turn around and walk away so I could check out the back view. As I watched he moved his hand to his shoulder and he began to knead the muscles there like he was tense.

I suddenly realized I was standing there, staring at him and not saying anything. I tried to rewind our conversation in my head. I'd been so busy staring at him…what the hell had I said? Thanks, I think? Okay, yes, I'd told him thanks for getting my dinner. What now? He wasn't saying anything either. Just standing there looking at the ground and rubbing his shoulder. What should I do next? I was saved from figuring it out when he raised his head, looked at me with his dark eyes, and started to talk.

Chapter 4

Dante

"Hey, I'm sorry I was like that last night. You just caught me on a bad day and..." She didn't make a sound, didn't move. Just looked at me with those pretty brown eyes. I knew I'd been standing there not saying anything. I'd been caught off guard by my reaction to her. How had I not noticed last night how beautiful she was? I guess you would call her beauty understated. It wasn't blatant like some women's. It didn't hit you in the face. But now that I'd had a minute to really look at her, it had knocked me off my game. And dammit, I was just standing there not saying anything again. I tried a smile and started again.

"Could we start over? Like we've never met?" I held out my hand for her to shake, not at all sure that she wasn't going to just take a step back and quietly close the door in my face. "Hi, I'm Dante. I live in 4B."

She looked at me another moment then took a breath and reached out her hand. "Mia. I'm Mia. I'm in 4A. Obviously."

I smiled again as she rolled her eyes at herself. Her small smile and pink cheeks were the prettiest thing I'd seen in a while. Her soft hand in mine felt good. So good I didn't want to let go. After a quick, gentle shake she started to draw her hand back and I forced myself to let her go. I didn't want her thinking I was some kind of creep just when she had apparently decided that I wasn't going to attack her. The way she'd looked at me and frozen last night when I came toward her, I was lucky she was still standing there with her door open and not quickly locking herself in, and me out, again.

"Hi, Mia. I don't think I thanked you for making sure that mail got to me." It hadn't turned out to be anything important, but she hadn't known that and besides, that wasn't the point. Some people would have just dumped it in the trash.

Her small smile returned at my thanks. "You're welcome. It was no trouble." She didn't continue and I wracked my brain for something else to say. Now that she was talking to me, I didn't want her to stop. I had no idea why, but I wasn't ready to lose her attention just yet.

"Um…have you lived here long? I just moved in a little over a month ago so I haven't met many people in the complex yet."

She tilted her head as if she was thinking. "I've lived here about 2 years, I guess? This is going to sound terrible, but I haven't met most of the people in the building either." She shook her head, looking amused. "Except for Mrs. Curr on the first floor. Watch out for her. She keeps a really, really close eye on where you park and how many visitor spots you use. She's the self-appointed parking lot monitor. If she thinks you've made an infraction, you'll hear about it."

"Okay, thanks." I smiled a little at the mental image of a cranky old lady bitching at me because my truck was parked too close to the lines. It was a monster, so it was bound to happen. "I'll do my best to obey the rules." I realized I was keeping her standing in her doorway, holding her dinner. She was probably wishing I would move along but she seemed too polite to say it.

"Well, I'll let you get to your dinner." I stepped backward, though I really wanted to go the other direction towards her. I didn't know what it was about this girl, but it was like she was a magnet pulling me closer. "It was good to meet you, Mia."

There was that soft, sweet smile again. "Good to meet you, too, Dante." I liked how my name sounded when she said it. "See you around."

I lifted my hand in a half wave as I backed toward my door. Mia stepped into her apartment and closed the door. I heard the locks turn and was glad. I'd definitely be keeping an eye out for her from across the way – what could I say, I had a protective streak a mile wide – but it was good that she was doing the basics to keep herself safe.

⌒

I didn't see Mia at all over the next two weeks. That wasn't surprising, I guess. I had only seen her twice before that and once was when I hijacked her dinner and knocked on her door. What did surprise me, though, was how much I had been hoping to see her. For one reason or another, she'd caught my attention and my brain wouldn't let go. I hadn't seen her, though, because I wasn't home much. I was keeping long hours at the gym because two of the kids I trained had competitions coming up. Between spending extra time with them and trying to make sure that I didn't neglect the other kids, I was practically living at the gym. Add in the fact that I was helping cover another trainer's adult clients while he was out after surgery, Pete was still bugging me, and I had the constant feeling that someone was watching me, and I was pretty stressed and exhausted. I was still in my early 30s but these days I was feeling old.

So it didn't help my mood any when I finally got home a little after 8pm – the earliest I'd made it home in weeks – and was met by the infamous Mrs. Curr in 1A. Mia had warned me and man, was she right. As expected, Mrs. Curr had plenty to say about both my truck – it was too big, too loud, too everything, apparently - and, in her opinion, my utter lack of ability to park within the confines of my designated space. Yes, the back bumper of my truck extended a bit beyond the lines of my parking spot. It was a big truck, there wasn't much I could do about it. It's not like I could magically make it shorter. Did I really need a truck that big? Probably not. But I was not a small guy and I needed my space. Besides, I liked it. Mrs. Curr clearly did not.

Though I'm sure the expression on my face probably wasn't the most pleasant, I managed to thank Mrs. Curr for the feedback politely and with only a little sarcasm. Hey, I did my best. I mentioned I was tired and stressed, right? The old bat was lucky I didn't tell her to fuck off and just keep walking, but my momma raised me to be respectful, especially to women, so like I said, I did my best.

Mia's door popped open just as I reached the landing for our floor. She had a full trash bag in her hand, so I assumed she was headed downstairs to the large trash bins.

"Hey, neighbor." Her soft voice and smile just did something to me.

"Hey, yourself." I sounded tired, even to me. "I just had my first run-in with the parking lot monitor. She's a real treat."

"Ouch." Mia winced. "She's something, isn't she? She's probably just lonely and doesn't have a lot to keep her attention, but…"

"You're a much nicer person than I am to think that way." I shook my head. My neck and shoulders were killing me, the muscles tight from too much stress and too many hours at the gym. I reached up and squeezed the back of my neck to try to loosen it up. "I think she's just a cranky busybody who likes to bitch at people."

Mia huffed out a quick breath that may have been a laugh. "Well, probably a little of that, too."

Mia watched me massage my neck for a few seconds, a little frown of concern on her face. "Are you okay? Did you hurt yourself?"

Her concern for me felt good. "No, not really. Just some tight muscles from too much work and not enough sleep." I dropped my hand and gave her a quick smile to show her I was okay, but she just continued to look at me like she was considering something. I was just about to ask her what was up when she spoke up and surprised the hell out of me.

"I could maybe help." After she spoke, Mia looked at the ground, shifting around like she was nervous.

"I...what?" Okay, I sounded like an idiot but I couldn't imagine...?

Mia took a deep breath, squared her shoulders, and looked up at me. She looked...determined, as if she'd made an important decision.

"Not maybe. I could definitely help. I used to do massage. It's been a couple of years but I'm sure I can still do it. It really helps with sore, stiff muscles. You could try a muscle relaxer, too, or ibuprofen of course, but massage can often help when nothing else does and wow, here I am talking like I'm your doctor or something. I'm sorry. I'll shut up now."

She ducked her head again. She looked like she regretted saying anything and hoped I would forget the whole thing. Not a chance.

"Massage? Really? You'd be willing to do that? I haven't had a massage since I was competing, but man I'd appreciate it. I hate muscle relaxers because they knock me on my ass and everything else only helps for a couple hours. That would be great, really." As I talked, she stopped memorizing the concrete under our feet and looked back up at me. For a second I thought she might tell me to forget it, she'd changed her mind, but luckily, I was wrong.

"Okay, good. Fine. That's fine." She was clearly nervous, maybe worried she'd forget what to do? "Um...when...what works for you?"

"Right now, maybe? Does that work? I don't have any plans tonight." A look of surprise crossed her face and I felt a little bad for jumping on her offer like that. But the pain was bad enough that it was making it hard to sleep. If I could get her help tonight, I'd take it.

"Oh sure. Yeah. That'll work. Just give me a few minutes to take my trash downstairs and dig out my massage chair. And wash my hands. Because, trash. I mean, I'd wash them anyway, but..." She stopped and closed her eyes. She took a breath, opened her eyes again, and said, "Right. See you in a few minutes" then headed for the steps.

Chapter 5

Mia

Oh my God, what was wrong with me? Why could I not have a conversation with this man without babbling like an idiot? He was just my neighbor, just a guy! Okay, an insanely hot, built, handsome, seemingly hard-working, decent – and did I mention hot? – guy, but still. I was 24, not 14! I should be able to have a normal conversation with a guy. And what the hell had I been thinking to offer to give him a massage? I could barely talk to the man, how the hell was I going to put my hands on him and not collapse into a pile of nerves? Under normal circumstances I wouldn't be worried about it. I was trained in massage and had worked on lots of people, male and female, even some athletes in great shape, with no concerns and no issues. But my reactions to Dante were anything but normal. I wasn't worried about my skills coming back to me. I knew they would. I was worried about touching him and staying professional. Well, you just will, I thought to myself. You offered, now you have to deliver.

I ran down the stairs, dumped my trash, and rushed back up to my apartment. Luckily my bedroom closet was just big enough that I'd been able to stuff my massage chair in the back when I moved in and forget about it. I hadn't had a need for it since then, but I'd kept it because you never knew. Yes, I'd decided to take a different direction when I'd moved here, but I figured I could always fall back on massage if I needed or wanted to.

I positioned the chair in the living room and headed to the bathroom to get some lotion. I didn't have massage oil on hand anymore, but I needed something to use for this impromptu massage, so unscented hand lotion would have to do. On my way back to the living room I heard a knock on my door. My stomach and heart both jumped. I gave myself a quick mental pep talk and went and opened the door. Dante stood outside in a different t-shirt and jeans. He'd obviously had time to take a shower and change in the five minutes I'd been rushing around like crazy. With my long hair, five-minute showers were a joke. Men had it so easy.

I said hi to Dante and stepped back to let him in. He walked past me, smelling so good that I sighed a little before I could catch myself. Hot, nice, and he smelled good. The universe wasn't fair. Whatever sound I'd made Dante must have heard it because he looked over his shoulder at me.

"Everything ok?"

"Oh sure. Yes. Fine. Just thinking about how to start." Yep, I was starting out great. I had this whole thing under control. I mentally rolled my eyes at myself and told myself to get a grip. "Have you had a seated massage before?" Good, that sounded calm, like I knew what I was doing. "I know some people prefer to lie on a table but I only have a chair here."

Dante moved toward the chair, not looking phased at all. "Sure, seated is fine. I've had that before. Whatever works for you. I just appreciate it."

"Okay, good. You know what to do then. Go ahead and take your shirt off and get comfortable. I'll be right back. I'm going to grab a bottle of water. Do you want one?"

"No, I'm okay. Thanks."

Out of the corner of my eye I could see Dante pulling his shirt over his head as I headed to the kitchen for a bottle of water that, in reality, I didn't need. What I needed was a second to compose myself. Focus, Mia. It was just a massage. I'd done hundreds of massages. Dante wasn't even the most attractive guy I'd ever worked on. I stepped out of the kitchen, saw Dante seated on the massage chair, shirt off as instructed, his broad, tan back facing me. Yeah, that was a lie. Dante was by far the hottest guy I'd ever worked on. It wasn't even that his face was stunningly handsome in a classic way. With his short dark hair and dark eyes he was certainly attractive and he had a great body. But really it was the whole package. He was compelling. His presence commanded your attention without him trying. And he had to be wondering what the hell I was doing just standing there, saying nothing. Time to give him the help I'd promised.

"Okay, looks like we're ready to go. Neck and shoulders, correct?" Dante nodded. "Do you mind the music I have on?" I'd turned on a playlist when I got home earlier and hadn't even realized it was playing in the background until just then. "I can turn it off."

"No, it's fine." Dante's voice was a little muffled because of his position on the massage chair, but he sounded relaxed and comfortable. That was a good start.

"Okay, one last question, then I'll stop asking you stuff and get started. I don't have any massage oil but I need to use something so I grabbed some unscented lotion. Is that okay to use? I promise you won't smell like a girl or anything."

Dante's shoulders moved a little as he chuckled. "Works for me if it works for you."

"Alright then, time to get this show on the road." Yes, I really said that. Out loud. Very smooth.

Rubbing a generous amount of lotion on my hands, I started my massage routine. "In just a minute you'll feel my hands on your shoulders. They might be a little bit cool from the lotion – sorry, the massage oil usually warms them up. Let me know if you need to stop at any point. Here we go."

I stepped forward bit and put my hands on Dante's shoulders right along either side of his neck. I suspected that's where his muscles were tightest based on what he'd said and the way he'd been rubbing his neck earlier. Dante tensed just a bit when my hands touched his shoulders, but quickly relaxed again. I kept my hands still for a moment letting him adjust to my touch, then began pressing lightly but firmly against his muscles to assess what was needed. His skin was warm and smooth under my hands. And his muscles were bunched up hard as stone. From his neck across his shoulders and along the upper part of his back I could feel his muscles tight and rigid.

"Wow, you weren't kidding. No wonder you're in pain."

"Yeah, it's been bad for a while. I should have done something sooner, but..." Dante's voice trailed off as I dug my thumbs in with just a bit of pressure, testing.

"Well, this should help a lot. I'm not going to able to fix it completely tonight and I can't promise it won't hurt some, but I'll try to warn you when I think it might."

"Go ahead and hurt me. I can take it." I could hear the grin in

Dante's voice even though I couldn't see it.

"Okay, tough guy. Here we go." Time to get serious. It was going to take all the strength I had in my hands to work out some of these knots. My hands and arms were sure to be killing me tomorrow especially since I hadn't done a massage in so long. But I was determined to help Dante as much as I could.

I concentrated on Dante and got to work. My focus narrowed to his muscles and his breathing and everything else faded away. I kneaded and pressed and watched and listened for any shifting or changes in his breathing to indicate if I hit a sensitive spot. I occasionally warned him softly, "This might hurt" when I came to a spot or used a technique that clients sometimes found painful. Dante never flinched and the only sounds he made were in response the couple of times I asked if he was doing okay. I got a grunt each time that I took as a "yes."

I worked on him as long as I could. I could still feel some spots that hadn't relaxed yet, but my hands and arms were toast. "I think that's all I can do tonight. How does that feel? Any better?"

"So much better. Better than I have in a long time." Dante sat back on the seat of the chair and stretched, lifting his arms above his head. I forced myself to look away as his muscles rippled.

"Good. That's good. I couldn't get all of the knots out, but at least it should help."

"It does and I really, really appreciate it." Dante stood up and reached for the shirt where it lay on the arm of my couch. "How can I thank you?" He pulled his shirt over his head and faced me, running his hands over his hair like he was fixing it, not that it was long enough to mess up.

I shook my head. "You already have. You feel better. That's all the thanks I need."

"No, seriously…"

"Really, I mean it. I was happy to do it."

Dante stood looking at me with narrowed eyes as if he was thinking.

"And hey, you bought me dinner the other night," I reminded him.

He shook his head even as I was saying it. "No, that wasn't a thank you. That was an apology. Doesn't count."

"Really, you don't have to do anything. I wasn't even able to work out your worst spots. You're still tensed up in places."

Now he stood with his hands on his hips, looking at me like I was talking nonsense.

"You can't seriously believe that matters to me. You helped me feel better than I have in weeks. You didn't have to help at all. Like I said, I really appreciate it and I will find a way to thank you."

I knew I shouldn't say what I was about to next, but I just hated that I hadn't been able to finish the job. Whether that was professional pride speaking or just plain stubbornness I wasn't sure, but I heard myself say, "Fine then, if you insist on thanking me, I need to finish the job. Give me a few days for my hands and arms to recover and then I'll work on getting those other knots out of your back."

Dante's eyes widened as I mentioned my hands and arms. "Oh fuck, I'm..."

"No." I cut him off. I didn't know where shy Mia had gone tonight but I was going with it. "No apologies. I offered and I was glad to do it. And I want to finish, period. Well, that's up to you of course, really. But no apologies."

Now he looked at me with a mixture of what looked like amusement and resignation on his face.

"I'm not going to win, am I?"

"Not this time."

"Okay." Dante shook his head. "I appreciate it...again. Just let me know what works for you. And I'm sorry, I won't apologize anymore."

I just caught the mischief in his eyes and the grin starting on his face as he turned toward the door. "Goodnight, Mia."

I couldn't stop my own answering smile. "Goodnight, Dante."

Chapter 6

Dante

When I woke up, I immediately realized two things. One, I'd actually slept instead of shifting around all night to get comfortable and two, I felt better than I had in a while. Yeah, there were a couple of spots that were still knotted up but nowhere near what there had been. The massage from Mia had me feeling great. The weird thing was the massage helped, yeah, but a big part of feeling better was just being around Mia. There was something about that girl. She had a strange effect on me, like she relaxed me and revved me up at the same time.

I laughed when I thought about how she said I still had tense spots after the massage. Little did she know she was talking about my dick when she said that. I'd gone hard the second her hands touched my skin. I had to talk myself down, the combination of her touch, her scent, her sweet voice and the feel of her so close to me making it hard in more ways than one. I hadn't been with a girl in a while – not since my bitch of an ex-girlfriend, Haven, showed herself to be the lying snake she was. Maybe I just needed to get laid, but I didn't think that was it. Sure, Mia was hot as fuck, but it was more than that. Thank God I'd put on jeans when I showered and changed before heading over to Mia's last night. If I'd had on sweats or basketball shorts there would have been no hiding my hard-on. As it was after the massage, I'd thrown my shirt on as quick as possible and just hoped Mia didn't look down. The fact that she'd offered to give me another massage in a couple days hadn't helped matters. Though I felt like shit that she'd worked her hands and arms so much that they'd been sore, my dick was apparently more focused on the fact that she had essentially volunteered to put her hands on me again. It didn't matter how much I reminded myself – and my dick – that she was just being a nice neighbor and trying to help, she was a trained professional, it wasn't an offer to hook up – yeah, my dick and the rest of my body, even my brain, weren't getting the message. All I could think about was getting my hands on her, what it would feel like to slip inside her. I felt myself grow harder thinking about how soft she'd be, how good she'd feel. I groaned, rolled out of bed, and headed for the bathroom. If I wasn't going to be in pain for the rest of the day, I had some business to take care of in the shower before I left for the gym.

In the bathroom, I turned on the shower then stripped off the boxer briefs I'd slept in. As the water warmed, I stepped in the shower and soaped up my hands. As I ran them over my body, my mind went back to Mia's hands on me. I reached down and gripped my steel hard dick, sliding my hand slowly from the base to the tip. Fuck, I was so close already from just thinking about Mia. This wasn't going to take long. I turned to face the shower head and let the water hit me in the chest as I stroked my dick. I pictured Mia's pretty brown eyes as she looked up at me, her pink lips tight around my aching dick. I pulled harder and reached down with my other hand for a light tug on my balls just like I liked. Not a minute later I felt my balls start to draw up and my dick swelled. I grunted as I came hard, cum splashing my stomach and chest for a second before rising away. Damn. If it was that good with my own hand, how much better would it be if I ever got to be inside Mia? I gave myself a few seconds to breathe, then finished up my shower and got dressed. A couple minutes later, I headed out the door with a protein bar and a mug of coffee. If the start was any indication, this was going to be a great day.

Ten hours later I was wishing I'd just said fuck it and stayed in bed to jack off to thoughts of Mia. The day had been shitty from the second I hit the gym. It started with a water leak in the men's locker room. Luckily, we caught it before it did too much damage and the repair wasn't major, but there was still a huge fucking mess to clean up. That didn't help Dev's already pissy mood. Apparently, he and his girl, Nicole, were fighting. Considering they'd only lived together for 2 months, that was a problem. Dev and I had been roommates before he decided to move Nicole in and I'd moved out. He might be regretting it, but I wasn't. If I hadn't moved, I wouldn't be neighbors with Mia now and that was turning out to be something I was pretty happy about. But with Dev's mood it sucked to be anywhere near him. Then Miles, one of my fighters who was getting ready for a competition in a couple of weeks, had shown up to the gym sick and I'd had to send him home. It wasn't the kid's fault he was sick – shit happened – but it would set us back on our training schedule if he didn't recover quick. And now Kenan, my most talented fighter who would also be competing in a couple weeks, was acting like a whiny little bitch. His focus was shit and he was half-assing his workout. I didn't have time for this. "Kenan, stop!" I finally yelled when I couldn't take watching him anymore. "What the fu...what is wrong with you today?" I did my best not to cuss when I was working with the kids. Some of them didn't have the best home lives and heard enough of that coming at them every day. They shouldn't have to hear it at the gym, too. But that didn't mean I took it easy on them.

"You got somewhere better to be? Something better to be thinking about than kicking your opponent's ass?" Oops, okay, so a cuss word or two still sometimes slipped out.

"Yeah, maybe I do! Maybe there are other things that are more important! Fuck it, who cares, I'm done."

Kenan tore at his gloves as he turned away from the bag he'd been working on. Kenan was the steadiest kid in the gym, so his outburst took me by surprise. I took a few steps forward and planted myself in his way. Kenan was 14 and a big kid for his age, but still way smaller than me. He pulled up short as I stepped in front of him, still calm enough, I guess, to realize that it would be a bad idea to try to push past me. He glared up at me and I laid a hand on his shoulder.

"Kenan, dude, what's going on? You've trained really hard to get where you are. What's this about?"

Kenan glared at me a second longer then his shoulders and his eyes dropped. "I don't know if I want to be a fighter anymore."

I tried not to let my surprise show on my face or in my voice. "Okay. Why not?"

"There's this girl at school. I like her, like a lot. I thought she liked me, too, but when she found out I was a fighter..." Kenan swallowed hard and shifted his eyes to the wall. Obviously, whatever had happened had hit him hard.

"When she found out you were a fighter?" I prompted him.

"She told me it was disgusting." Kenan's eyes met mine, his filled with pain and disappointment. "She said it was brutal and violent. That she didn't want anything to do with it. Or me."

Well, fuck. Poor kid. It was nothing I hadn't heard before – many, many times – but it was never easy to hear something you loved talked about in that way. Especially by people who knew nothing about the sport and who really had no idea what they were talking about. But this was a tough one. This girl was obviously important to Kenan.

"Does this girl have a name?"

"Yeah, Jasmine."

"Have you tried talking with Jasmine at all about boxing? Telling her about all the training you do, how much you love it? That's it not just hitting people to hit them?"

"She didn't give me a chance. Just looked at me like I was dirt and walked away. She won't talk to me now." Kenan's shoulders slumped in defeat.

"Look, man, I'm sorry that happened. It sucks and I get it. Sometimes it can be hard for people to understand. Some people will just never get it or just never like it. That's the way it is. If you really like this girl, you have to try to talk to her. Tell her what you love about boxing, what got you into it. If she listens and changes her mind or at least gives it a chance, then great. But if she doesn't, man, if she doesn't want to know about something that's such a big part of who you are, maybe she's not the girl for you."

"Yeah, I guess. Sucks, though." Kenan rolled his shoulders and finally nodded. "I'll try to talk to her tomorrow."

"Alright, are we good now? Ready to get back to business?"

"Yeah, I gotta leave by eight, though. Gotta get my sister at the library when it closes." Kenan often had responsibility for his younger sister when his mom was at work, so this was nothing different.

"No time to waste then. Hit the bag, then the ropes, and finish with sprints." Kenan groaned, but got moving. It was a hard finish to what had been a long workout, but I wasn't going to go soft on him now. He had the potential to be a great fighter, but he had to decide whether he had it in him to commit to it, all distractions aside.

⁓

The next day didn't get much better. I was running late to the gym because I forgot to set my alarm, but I got through the morning class and individual clients without any issues. My luck ran out there. Pete was waiting for me when I stepped out of the gym for a minute to grab some lunch at the deli two doors down. I nearly went right back into the gym to avoid him, but I was afraid he'd just follow me. Better to give him time to say whatever was on his mind so I could get back to work.

"Dante, man, it's been a while. Where ya been?" Pete was a slight, skinny guy with rounded shoulders and stringy hair. He never stood still, he was constantly fidgeting, twitching, moving around. I didn't think he was on anything, he just seemed like a twitchy, nervous guy. I could deal with it for a few minutes, after that I knew it would start to get on my nerves. Pete wasn't a bad guy, really, he was just kind of hard to be around. Maybe I was a dick for saying that, but I tried to at least be polite to him when he showed up. Unfortunately, a lot of other people were anything but polite.

"It's only been a couple weeks, Pete. I've been working. You know that's all I do."

As he followed me into the deli, Pete laughed like I'd told a great joke. I had no idea why. I stepped up to the counter to order my lunch, moved over to the register to pay for it, and then stood and waited, Pete still sticking by my side. It was probably rude not to ask him if he wanted something to eat but my politeness where he was concerned didn't go that far. If I thought he was going hungry, that would be one thing. But I knew he lived with his older sister in a little house not too far from my apartment. The house was older, but it and the yard were kept up, so it seemed like they were probably doing okay. Likely that was thanks to Pete's sister rather than Pete. I had no idea what Pete did for money.

"Yeah, that's you. All work, no play, huh? No hot chicks? No action going on?" Pete picked right up where he'd left off. As if I'd tell him if I did have something going on. Not that I did. Mia flashed into my head for a second, but she was way more than a "hot chick" and there was no way in hell Pete needed to know anything about her.

"You know I have no time for chicks, Pete." I grabbed my order as the woman handed it over the counter. I headed back to the gym and Pete followed me out. "I have to get back to work. See you around." I reached for the door of the gym, but Pete's hand on my arm stopped me.

"Wait, D." I hated it when Pete called me D. I stood and looked at Pete's hand, not moving, until he finally got the hint and removed it. I looked at him but said nothing. I knew what was coming next. I'd thought I might be able to avoid this today, but...

"Have you thought any more about getting back in the ring? I still have those backers who are real interested in seeing you fight Miller again, you know, gettin' that title back and shuttin' his mouth good for him." Pete seemed excited, like this fight had any chance of happening. Which it didn't.

"Pete, no. I've told you this plenty of times before. I haven't thought about it because it's not happening. I'm done. I don't compete anymore. I haven't in over a year. I don't give a shit about Justin Miller or his big mouth. Fuck him. Tell your backers to find someone else."

Now Pete looked agitated, like he couldn't believe what I was saying. Like he hadn't heard the same thing from me before.

"Fuck him, huh? Well, Haven sure is, isn't she?"

I turned to look at Pete, making sure he saw that I was deadly serious about what I said next. "He's welcome to her. They're the perfect couple. And it's time for you to go." I walked through the door, half hoping he would follow me because I needed something to hit right then, but also knowing I'd feel like shit if I hit Pete. Showing more brains than I thought he had, or maybe it was just survival instinct, he didn't follow me. My stomach churning, I walked into the small staff break room and threw my lunch in the fridge. No way I was going to eat it now. Not when thoughts of my former rival and my bitch of an ex-girlfriend were swirling in my head.

I hit the treadmill for a few hard miles, playlist blasting in my ears, until it was time for the first of the kids to start showing up for the afternoon. There was a youth beginner class to handle and then my teen fighters to work with. They kept me busy and focused, all my rage from earlier dimmed down to merely being pissed off that I'd had to think about those two at all.

That was until Dev pulled me aside late in the evening, a serious look on his face.

"Before you head out tonight, I need a minute."

"Sure, but what's up? That look on your face has me worried." Dev was never exactly cheerful but he looked kind of...grim.

"Nothing to worry about, just something you should know before word starts getting around. Finish up with the kids. It can wait." I stared at Dev's back for a couple seconds as he walked away, then turned around and did what he said. I put Kenan and Miles through one last drill, then told them to cool down. Kenan had been a lot more settled today, so things must have gotten better with his girl. Miles was still dragging a little from being sick, but we were easing back into it. I started cleaning up for closing, figuring Dev would come find me when he was ready.

It didn't take long for Dev to reappear out of the office. We said good night to Kenan and Miles as they headed out, leaving me, Dev, and Kelsey, our lone female trainer, in the gym.

Dev called out to Kelsey across the gym where she was finishing up sanitizing the mats. "Hey, Kels, go ahead and go on home now. I know you have class early. We'll get things cleaned up." Kelsey was still in school, studying physical therapy. She called back her thanks, went to get her bag from the break room, and waved goodbye as she left the gym.

"Okay, you got everybody out, now what's up?" Whatever he had to say, I just wanted him to get to it already so I could go home and crash. Yesterday had sucked and today hadn't been much better.

"Miller and Haven are back in the area. I just found out today."

And that just put a cap on this fucking day.

"Fuck, fuck, fuck!" No kids were around now so no reason not to say what I felt. "Why are they back? Do you know?" They'd been in Vegas for almost a year. Why had they come back now? Why had they come back at all?

"I have no idea. I don't know that there is a specific reason. They weren't gonna stay in Vegas forever."

"No, I guess not. Damn, shit, fuck. I do not want to have to deal with this right now." I could feel the knots Mia had worked out the other night starting to bunch up again.

"Just because they're back doesn't mean you'll run into them. They won't wander out this way, they'll stay in the city. They're too big time for a couple of has-been fighters like us," Dev finished with a laugh.

I had to laugh, too. No doubt there were fans and others who considered both Dev and me has-beens. I considered us guys who had trained hard, fought hard, achieved what we set out to, and then moved on. We had both dreamed of being championship boxers and we'd both achieved that. We'd never competed against each other – Dev was a higher weight class and a few years older than me – but we'd known each other most of our lives. Dev's uncle had raised him and trained him in the same gym we were standing in now. When his uncle died in his sleep a few months after Dev won his title, he'd walked away from competition to take over the gym and to be there for the aunt who, along with his uncle, had raised him like her own son. A few years later, I'd had my own reasons for calling it quits after winning my own title and achieving the goals I'd set out for myself.

Dev had reached out right away to see if I was interested in helping to set up a youth program at his gym. That had been about a year ago and we had a solid program up and running. We both had a lot to be proud of. So if some people thought we were has-beens I really couldn't find it in myself to care. Which brought my mind back around to my two least favorite people in the world – Justin Miller and Haven Day. They considered me not only a has-been, but a coward and a fool. I considered them lying, cheating scum. I didn't like to say that I hated anyone, but the intense dislike and lack of respect was definitely mutual. Dev was right, though. We were far enough away from the city that there was no reason to run into them. Whatever the reason they were back from Las Vegas it had nothing to do with me, so there was no reason to stress about them being back. If only I could tell that to the knots in my neck and shoulders that were definitely back in force.

⌒

I pulled into my spot in the apartment complex parking lot, glad that this day was over. I wanted a hot shower, a cold beer, and mindless sports on my huge TV, in that order. I massaged my neck and thought for two seconds about having Mia's hands on me as she worked out the rest of the knots. As good as that sounded, I was in a crap mood and didn't want to take the chance it would spill over on her. She didn't deserve it and I didn't want to ruin the friendly neighbor vibe we had going on. I liked Mia and I didn't want to give her any reason to scurry back in her apartment and hide from me again.

As if thinking about Mia had made her appear, I turned the corner to head up the stairs and there she was. She was standing and talking with none other than Mrs. Curr. Mia was wearing what looked a uniform, her hair up, a purse and bag hanging from her shoulder. It looked like she was just getting home from work. I'd never seen her hair up before. It looked good, the color seeming darker than the golden-brown color it was when it was down. Little curls escaped along her neck and made me want to put my mouth on her there. As I got closer, I realized that Mrs. Curr was giving Mia shit over some car she'd seen in the parking lot earlier.

"It was parked in your visitor spot. Just sitting there with the engine running, polluting the air." Mrs. Curr looked up at Mia sternly, frown on her face. "The music was so loud the windows rattled," she continued, making it clear she thought this was somehow Mia's responsibility.

"I'm sorry whoever it was disturbed you, Mrs. Curr, but I don't know anyone who drives a silver car with tinted windows. They must have parked in my spot by mistake." Mia looked up at me as I stopped next to her. Her voice was soft and calm, as always. She was obviously trying to be polite to Mrs. Curr, but I could see just the slightest hint of irritation in her eyes. Her eyes looked tired, too, like she'd had a long day. It must be going around.

"Good evening, Mrs. Curr," I said in the friendliest tone I could muster. "It's too bad people can't be more respectful, but the people in that car could have been looking for anyone who lives in the complex."

Mrs. Curr somehow managed to look down her nose at me while also having to look up a fair distance to transfer her frown to me. It was a neat trick actually. I wondered if she practiced that in her mirror.

"Speaking of respectful, young man, your ability to park within your assigned space hasn't improved. It's blatantly disrespectful and rude to the other residents." She sniffed and tilted her nose even higher, looking very self-righteous. "I've a mind to speak to the management about it."

I felt my blood pressure start to rise. With all the frustration I'd had the past 2 days, the last thing I needed was this cranky old lady busting my balls over parking. "I have an end spot in the back corner of the lot. I'm not blocking anyone or taking up anyone else's space." My irritation was clear in my voice, but I was done being polite. This woman needed to find something better to do with her time. "If you want to talk about being rude..."

Mia shifted slightly so that she stood a bit in front of me. Her shoulder pressed lightly into my chest as she leaned back into me a bit. Feeling her pressed against me, even just that light touch, dampened my irritation with Mrs. Curr. The urge to wrap my arms around Mia and pull her more fully against me took its place. I breathed in the light scent of her shampoo and felt my pulse begin to settle. "Dante's truck really isn't a problem, Mrs. Curr. It's not in anyone's way. He's very considerate." I knew Mia was just trying to defuse the situation a bit but having her stand up for me in the process felt pretty great. I felt Mia's hand slip around my forearm as she started nudging me toward the stairs. "Now it's been a long day and we won't take up anymore of your time." As if we'd been the ones to stop Mrs. Curr rather than the other way around. "Good night, Mrs. Curr."

Mia turned around and started toward the stairs, pulling me along like she was afraid I might resist. I followed, more than willing to be done with the encounter with our irritating neighbor. I heard a "humph!" from Mrs. Curr as we walked away, but I didn't hear anything more. Apparently, she wasn't willing to chase us up the stairs to continue her tirade.

Mia dropped her hand from my arm as we started to climb the stairs. When we reached our floor, she turned to me, amusement lighting up her tired eyes. "What ever would we do without Mrs. Curr keeping watch over our parking lot? Now I'm getting in trouble for people I don't even know parking in my spot when I'm not even here!" Mia laughed and I found myself chuckling a little along with her. Mia's laugh was hard to resist. "And you, young man..." Mia looked at me with mock sternness, "you are not Mrs. Curr's favorite person. I thought you were going to have a throwdown with her for a second," she said, clearly teasing.

I groaned, tilting my head back and closing my eyes. "I know." I lowered my head again and met Mia's eyes. "Thanks for stepping in and getting us out of there. I know I shouldn't let her get to me. Today is just not the day."

"Yeah, I can tell you're a little stressed." Mia nodded at my hand massaging my neck. I hadn't even realized I'd been doing that. I dropped my hand as she went on. "My hands have recovered from the other night. Why don't I finish your massage tonight?"

The thought of having Mia's hands on me again, and maybe even being able to sleep tonight without my shoulders in knots, sounded amazing but..."Naw, I'll take a rain check if that's okay. I've had a shit day and I'm in a shit mood. I wouldn't be good company. I can tell your day was a long one, too. You look tired."

Her eyes, though undeniably tired, lit up with amusement again. "Why Dante, you charmer. That's just what every woman wants to hear."

She was smiling, but seriously, what the fuck was wrong with me? It was true, she looked tired, but no less beautiful than she ever did. "Shit, I'm sorry, I didn't mean it that way."

"Dante, I'm teasing. I know I look tired. I *am* tired. But not too tired to work those knots out. Come on. You'll feel better and it will help both of us take our mind off our bad day." I could feel myself waffling. She was hard to resist and she really seemed to want to do it. "You don't have to be good company. You don't even have to talk. I'll just put some music on again. You chatted my ear off last time so this will be a nice change." I couldn't help but chuckle at her teasing grin. Where had my shy little neighbor gone? We both knew I'd barely said a word last time. What she didn't know was that I'd spent the whole time enjoying the feel of her hands on me and trying to talk my hard-on down. I didn't expect this time to be any different.

I gave in. "Okay, you convinced me." She looked like that made her happy and the fact that I'd put that look on her face made me happy. I was quickly getting in over my head with this girl, but that obviously wasn't stopping me. "Just let me take a quick shower and I'll be over."

Seven minutes later I was walking into her apartment. Mia stepped back as she let me in and I noticed that she'd changed but left her hair up.

"I've never seen your hair up before. It looks good that way."

"Oh yeah," she said, lifting a hand to it. "I changed quick and forgot it was still up. I usually take it down when I get home from work, but this way it won't get in the way during the massage, I guess."

I suddenly realized I knew next to nothing about Mia. Well, except for the fact that she was trained in massage, her touch did crazy things to me, and she wasn't afraid to face down a nosy old bat if it meant keeping me out of trouble. "Where do you work? I noticed what you were wearing earlier looked like it might be a uniform." As I spoke, I pulled my shirt off over my head and headed for the massage chair sitting in the middle of Mia's living room. I could hear her moving around the room as I sat down and made myself comfortable.

"I'm going to use the same lotion I did last time if that's okay?" I could feel Mia step close to me as I nodded. "Okay, here we go. You'll feel my hands." I was prepared for the feel of her hands on me this time and didn't tense at her touch. She pressed gently against my neck and shoulders for a few seconds, then got down to work, pressing in more firmly. "I'm a front desk supervisor at the hotel in the Tower Center downtown. You're right that I was wearing a uniform. We have several pieces that we can mix and match however we want. It gets boring but it makes getting ready for work easy."

I liked listening to Mia's voice and I wanted to keep her talking. Learning more about her was a bonus. "So, what was the long day about?"

"Two things really." Mia pressed and kneaded and worked my muscles as she spoke. It was painful and felt great at the same time. "We had a big tour group check-in tonight, which is always chaotic to some extent. They were a great group, very patient, but it's always a bit of a zoo getting that many people checked in at the same time." As Mia talked, she stopped periodically to put more lotion on her hands and to press her hands on me, testing for sore spots. "The other thing was that one of the front desk staff called off at the last minute, again. Everyone gets sick or has life happen sometimes, but Kurt…" she paused as she kneaded hard on a tough spot. She leaned in and I groaned as I felt the muscle finally relax under the firm pressure. She smoothed her hand over my skin and went on. "Kurt calls off all the time, and it really causes issues for the other front desk staff. Luckily this time I was there and able to stay to help get the tour group settled, but if I hadn't been it would have been a rough time for the staff who were there. And he's had a couple of complaints for being rude. Guests can be difficult, no question, and you don't have to let them get abusive, but you can't get rude. I've talked with him, but things haven't gotten better. I think I'm going to have to let him go. That's never easy but given his personality, its sure to be really unpleasant. And here I am yammering away when I told you we didn't have to talk."

"No, you said *I* didn't have to talk." I knew my voice was muffled from my face-down position on the chair, but she seemed to understand me well enough. "You talking is just fine. I like hearing about your day."

"Oh yes, the exciting life of hotel front desk staff." I could hear the smile in her voice. "Actually, when I think about it, I do have some funny stories. Not nearly as many as the housekeeping staff, but some of the stories they tell are not things I want to see with my own eyes. People do some crazy things."

"I'd love to hear those stories some time. How long have you worked there?"

"Just about two years. I got the job right after I moved here. I started on overnights, then worked my way to days, and then supervisor." Her hands paused and I felt her step back a bit. "How do you feel? Any spots still feel tight?"

I focused on the muscles in my neck, shoulders, and upper back and realized that they all felt warm and loose. There was just one spot – "There's one spot right along my spine." I nearly groaned as Mia's soft hand slid along my upper back. "Right there. It's just a little tight."

"I feel it." She stepped in closer again and pressed into the muscle. It took a few seconds but slowly it began to relax. She kept kneading it, making sure that the knot was completely gone. "Anywhere else?"

"No, I'm good." I sat back on the massage chair. "And you're magic. And I still haven't done anything to thank you."

"Ugh, don't start that again." Mia stepped away to set down the lotion as I grabbed my shirt and pulled it on. "There's nothing magic about me and no thanks are needed."

I stood and turned to face her, lifting my hands in defeat. "Alright, I'll be good." A few more strands of Mia's hair had come loose while she worked on me and it was all I could do not to reach out and see if they felt as silky as they looked. I'd love to show her just how "good" I could be. At least I'd managed to keep my dick under control this time, although thinking like that wasn't going to help.

"You know, with skills like yours I'm wondering why you're working at a hotel front desk. Unless that's your dream job or something. I can see you being good at just about anything."

"Thank you, that's a really nice thing to say. No, it's not my dream job but it will do for now."

We were done with the massage and I knew I should go, but I couldn't make myself walk over to the door. An hour ago, all I'd wanted was to be alone with a beer and sports on the TV. Now I wanted to stay here, talking with Mia, close to her and surrounded by her scent. What the hell was happening to me? I should be running for my apartment, but I couldn't pull myself away. Her eyes still looked tired though and I knew I had to get the hell out of her apartment and let her get some sleep.

I forced myself to move toward the door. "Not your dream job, huh? What is?"

Mia followed me, not rushing like she was eager to see me go, just moving in my direction. At my question, she laughed and shook her head. "I have no idea what my dream job is. I'm twenty-four with no idea what I want to be when I grow up. If I figure it out, I'll let you know."

I opened the door but didn't step through yet. "Twenty-four, huh? Well, you're still kind of a baby, so you have time yet." I couldn't help but smile as Mia started to laugh.

"A baby, huh? And how old are you, oh wise one?" I seriously couldn't believe this smiling, sarcastic girl was the same one who'd been so nervous she'd practically passed out the first time we met.

"I'm thirty-one."

"Wow, that old? You'd better toddle on home and get some sleep then. It must be way past your bed- time." Mia giggled – it was so fucking cute – and I couldn't help but laugh again. Had I ever had this much fun just being around a girl, just talking to her? If I had, I didn't remember it.

"Watch it, missy." I walked over, unlocked my door and turned to face Mia as I stepped inside. "Show respect for your elders."

"Yeah, you and Mrs. Curr!" Mia shut her door quickly, getting the last word and, literally, the last laugh.

Chapter 7

Mia

I woke up the next day when the sun hit my eyes. I was thankful I had the day off and was able to sleep in. It had taken me a long time to fall asleep the night before, thoughts of Dante filling my head. I'd talked his ear off last night, but it had helped distract me from how good his skin felt under my hands. As I had lain in bed trying to sleep, all I could think about was how good he looked with his shirt off. I mean, he was hot enough with it on, but with it off…holy mother, but the man was built. I knew he worked at a gym so maybe he was some kind of personal trainer? He'd mentioned competing in the past, but I couldn't recall that he'd mentioned a sport. Whatever it was, even though he'd apparently retired from competition, he was still in amazing shape. After tossing in my bed for over an hour, I'd finally reached in my nightstand drawer for my BOB. Imagining Dante over me, inside me, I came hard and fast. I just hoped I could look Dante in the eye the next time I saw him. I didn't feel shy around him anymore, but I'd never come saying his name before either.

I pushed the covers off and winced a bit at the stiffness in my hands. They weren't nearly as sore as the last time I'd given Dante a massage, and my arms weren't doing too bad either, but I was still glad I wouldn't be at work using a keyboard all day. Checking the clock, I saw that I had a few hours before I needed to head out to meet Meg for lunch. It had been too long since I had seen her, our busy schedules limiting most of our conversations to text messages. Just as I had the thought, I heard my phone ping with a new text.

Meg: Still on for lunch at 11:30? You better say yes.

I could almost hear Meg saying that. She could be such a smartass. I texted back one word.

Me: Yes.

Three little dots popped up right away.

Meg: Really or are you just saying that because I said you had to?

Me: Because you said I had to. I guess I was a smartass, too. *Kidding, kidding! We're on.*

Meg: Bitch. Okay if we meet at the new vegan place on Ferguson? I want to check it out and no one at work will go with me.

Yuck, vegan? Gee, why wouldn't everyone at Meg's work be rushing to check that out? The things I did for my best friend…

Me: Sure. That sounds…great.

Meg: You'll love it, wait and see. You liked that vegan chili I made.

Okay, she had a point. It was only one meal, maybe it wouldn't be so bad. Besides, I could mark it down as an accomplishment in my effort to get out there and try new things.

Me: Anything's possible. See you there at 11:30.

I spent the next few hours doing laundry and cleaning up my apartment. Before I knew it, it was time to head out the door to meet Meg. Why did days off always seem to go so much faster than days at work?

When I reached the restaurant, I was surprised to see how busy it was. It seemed popular so hopefully the food was good. As soon as I walked in the door, I heard Meg calling my name. I turned and saw her waving at me from a small table. There were two drinks already sitting on the table.

"Hey, I went ahead and ordered for both of us," Meg said as I slipped off my jacket and sat down. "It was so busy already when I got here that I was afraid to wait. If you hate what I got you, I'll pay for it."

"I'm sure it will be great." I'd actually settle for edible, but whatever.

"Let's hope. Now tell me what the hell you've been up to. Have you seen any more of that hot neighbor of yours…what was his name… Dante?"

I'd told Meg about meeting Dante and then about our first massage session. Of course I had, she was my best friend and I told her everything. But the thing about Meg was that when something caught her interest, she was relentless. And my "hot neighbor" as she called Dante, had very much caught her interest. I was half worried that she was going to show up at his door one day and demand to know his life story.

"Of course I've seen him, Meg. I live across the landing from him."

Meg gave me the look, the one that said to quit acting dumb and spill it. "I realize that Miss Smarty Pants. Have you spoken to him? Had your hands on him again? Details, woman, come on. You know I've got nothing going on in the man department. I have to live vicariously through you."

I shook my head. "It's not like that, Meg. We're just neighbors. It's not like I'm dating him or something."

"Not yet, but you have to start somewhere. Neighbors today, hot stud in your bed tomorrow."

She stopped as the server brought our food. She'd ordered me a black bean burger on a vegan bun and sweet potato fries. Meg knew I loved sweet potato fries so those were a safe bet. The burger didn't look half bad and it smelled really good. Meg had a salad with a bunch of veggies and grains. Not my thing, but she looked happy with it. She took a bite, nodded happily, and continued where she'd left off.

"So spill. Any more contact?"

I swallowed a bite of my surprisingly good burger. "Fine, yes. I gave him another massage last night." Meg's eyes widened but I cut off whatever she was about to say. "Remember I told you that my hands and arms were jelly before I got done the other night? Well, I told Dante that I would finish as soon as they recovered and I saw him last night and he was all tensed up again and we both had time, so yeah, I gave him another massage. He said thanks, I said you're welcome, and that was that." Okay, so that wasn't exactly true. I mean it was mostly true. But I left out the part about how we'd talked and laughed. I left out how much fun it was to be around him, how I forgot to be shy and nervous. It felt special somehow and I didn't want to dissect it with Meg, best friend or not.

"Really? That was that? No, hey we should get a drink together sometime, or hey, you should wake up in my bed after a long night of wild monkey sex sometime?"

"Geez, Meg. Keep your voice down." I glanced at the tables around us. Meg sometimes had no awareness that there were actually people around her who just maybe didn't need to hear her conversations. Luckily, it was pretty loud in the restaurant, so I didn't think anyone had overheard.

"No, none of that. Dante isn't interested in me that way, Meg. If you saw him, you'd understand. He's tall and gorgeous and confident as hell. He could have any girl he wants. He's not going to go for the shy, awkward girl who lives across the hall."

"You don't give yourself enough credit, Meems." Meg's nickname for me was ridiculous but she'd called me that since we were kids so I always let her get away with it. "Sure, you're a little shy but you're working on that and you've come a long way. Besides that, you're gorgeous. Yes, you are," she insisted as I shook my head. "You don't really see yourself, Mia, you can't, or you'd realize how beautiful you are."

"I love you for saying that and I'm sure you believe it, but that aside, Dante could snap his fingers and have girls come running. He's not only hot as hell, he's considerate. And funny. And nice." And based on the gleam in Meg's eyes I needed to stop talking before I dug the hole I was in any deeper.

"Oh, really?"

"Yes, really. And you know what else he is?"

"What?"

"Not interested in me, that's what." Meg rolled her eyes at me but thankfully let the subject of Dante drop.

"Fine, whatever. What are you up to on Friday?"

"Nothing. I work Friday, but nothing Friday night. Wait, unless you want me to go to hot yoga with you again. In that case, I'm busy. Completely booked up." Meg had talked me into joining her at an evening hot yoga class several weeks before and let's just say it hadn't gone well. Yoga was intimidating enough since I didn't practice regularly, but yoga in a blazing hot room? I'd survived, but just barely. Not even my love for Meg could convince me do that again.

"I know, I know, hot yoga sucks, blah, blah, blah. No, it's nothing like that. A bunch of us from the office are meeting up at that pub near your apartment. It's been a stressful quarter. We figured we'd blow off some steam and have a few drinks."

"I don't know, Meg. I don't really know your co-workers that well." I wasn't good at small talk, at chatting comfortably about...whatever...with people I'd just met. What other people called "networking" I called "torture". This wouldn't be a professional situation but still. The firm that Meg worked for was the biggest in this part of the country. Like Meg, her co-workers were all what my mom would call "big personalities" – dynamic, bold, and loud. To an introvert like me, they were a tough bunch to be around.

"This is the perfect chance to get to know them better." Meg finished her drink and set it aside. "They're fun people, Meg. They won't bite. And Mike will be there." She fiddled with the straw in her cup and glanced up as if checking my expression. "You remember him from the Derby party, right?"

"Yes, I remember him." Well, sort of. I remembered that he was about my height, attractive with hmm…light brown hair? He'd seemed okay, maybe a little overly impressed with himself, but I honestly hadn't spent much time with him. The Derby party had taken place at Meg's boss' house and I'd spent most of the time admiring the art and the beautiful gardens and slowly sipping my way through a truly awful Derby standard, a mint julep.

"He asked today if you would be with me Friday. He's interested in you, Mia. I can tell."

"You think so? Hmm." I wasn't sure how I felt about that. He seemed okay, as much as I could remember anyway. But there hadn't been any spark when he was near me. That, I would have remembered. I hadn't felt drawn to him, hadn't felt like I wanted to step closer like with… I stopped myself before I could finish that thought. This wasn't about Dante. He had nothing to do with this at all.

"Yes, I definitely think so. Come with me, Mia. It's just a few drinks. If you're not having fun, we can leave. We'll be right down the street from your apartment. You won't even have to leave your neighborhood. You promised to try to get out more, you know."

"Okay, okay, you win." It was easiest just to give in. And Meg was right, I had promised to get out more. I was twenty-four years old. A Friday night out at a pub meeting people for drinks was exactly the kind of thing I should be doing. I'd passed the pub a bunch of times and kept telling myself I'd go in sometime. This was my perfect chance. And maybe it would even be fun.

⁓

I kept repeating that to myself as I dug through my closet looking for something to wear Friday night. This would be fun, this would be fun, this would be fun.

I'd rushed home from work, showered, and dried my hair. Now I was standing in front of my closet in my short robe, rejecting outfit after outfit. I sighed. I couldn't find anything to wear because I didn't want to go. I was so pathetic. Here I was – young, single, ready to head out for a Friday night, with an attractive guy who was maybe probably interested in me waiting to spend time with me – and what I really wanted to do was put on my comfy sweats and plop on the couch. I wished that Meg was headed to my apartment with a bottle of wine like so many other Friday nights. I always had plenty of snacks in my apartment. We'd hang out, have snacks and wine, and I'd be perfectly happy.

Unfortunately, that wasn't what I had to look forward to tonight. Yeah, poor me, my best friend was forcing me to get out in the world and live a tiny bit. Sick of myself for being such a whiner about going out, I focused again on my closet. I pulled out a black top that I liked because it actually enhanced my small bust and a pair of jeans that Meg told me made my butt look good. I put on the top and jeans and added a black belt and black boots with kitten heels. Checking myself in my full-length mirror I gave myself a nod. Good enough. Heading to the bathroom I ran a brush through my hair, swiped on eyeliner, mascara, and lipstick, and I was ready to go.

Chapter 8

Dante

*M*y phone buzzed with a text just as I pulled into the parking lot at the gym. Thanks to Mia I felt much better both physically and mentally than I had in the past few days. Her massage had relaxed my muscles and had helped me get a full night sleep in comfort. And the time spent with her had cleared my mind and improved my mood. And jacking off in the shower to thoughts of her again hadn't hurt either. It was becoming a habit, but not one I necessarily wanted to break.

I shut off the truck and looked at my phone. The text was from my friend, Jamey.

Jamey: You still alive?

It had been forever since I'd talked to any of the guys. I'd been busy with work but that was no excuse.

Me: Yeah, sorry. Just crazy busy at work.

Jamey: Take a break and stop by the pub tonight. Cal's in town.

Cal, short for Callahan, was the twin brother of our other friend, Kendrick. They, Jamey, and I had all grown up together.

Kendrick and Cal owned Brothers Pub down the street from my apartment. Though Cal was part owner he was out of town a lot for his other job. Kendrick was the one who lived and breathed the pub. Jamey ran the kitchen. We'd all come a long way from where we'd grown up. We'd all had okay home lives for the most part, though

45

Jamey and his dad had locked horns constantly. We just hadn't grown up with much. We'd stuck together, more brothers than friends, and we'd made it. It would be great to see all the guys together.

Me: I'll be there.

As it worked out, I was able to get to the pub pretty early. Kenan had to leave early to get home for his sister so I was able to get home, shower, change, and walk the few blocks to the pub in time to walk through the door a little after 8pm. The fact that the pub was so close had been one of the things that had sold me on my current apartment. Dev lived all the way on the other side of town closer to the gym, so when I lived with him it was more of an effort to stop in the pub. Living so close was supposed to mean I'd be there more often but so far it hadn't worked out that way. I was glad to finally have a chance to hang out with the guys and have a few beers. And the fact that Cal was in town made it even better.

Cal's shout greeted me as soon as I walked through the pub's door. "Dante! About time you showed your ugly face in here."

I couldn't help but grin as he stood up from his bar stool as I headed toward him. Cal never changed – he was as loud and enthusiastic as ever. "I wouldn't be talking about ugly faces there, Junior." Cal was the younger of the twins by 17 minutes, making him the youngest of our group. He had taken many, many hours of ribbing due to that fact as we were growing up. He laughed at the childhood nickname as he grabbed me in a one-armed hug and pounded me on the back so hard that Kendrick, who was standing behind the bar, laughed.

"Damn Cal, are you saying hi or trying to kick his ass?"

Cal's grin just got bigger as he settled back on his bar stool. "Whatever works, man, whatever works."

I grabbed the stool that Cal had been saving for me. The pub wasn't packed yet, but it would be soon. Cal had saved me the stool at the end of the bar next to the wall. I had enough space to turn sideways on my stool and lean against the wall. Cal knew that I was never comfortable with my back to a crowded room, even in a familiar place. It was just a quirk of mine, I guess. In this spot I had plenty of room for my big frame and an easy view of most of the main room, including the door.

Kendrick poured me a beer, sliding it in front of me as soon as I sat down. No need to tell him what I was drinking. I'd sat at his bar many times. I took my first sip of the cold beer and it hit me how long it had been since I'd gotten to spend time with my friends. It had been way too long. Jamey was still back in the kitchen, but I knew he would step out to the front when he could.

"So, tell me all the news," Cal said. "You know how I hate being out of the loop."

I started filling Cal in on the details of my exciting – ha! – life and catching up with his. He traveled a lot as tour manager for an up and coming band, so he had much more interesting tales to tell than I did. Kendrick joined in between serving customers along with the other two bartenders. Jamey finally got a chance to step out of the kitchen, bringing with him huge burgers for me & Cal. I didn't normally eat much red meat – a habit left over from my training days – but Jamey's food was an exception. Anything he put in front of me, I ate. With his talent in the kitchen, I knew that whatever it was it would be amazing. His talent was really wasted cooking and running the kitchen in a little pub, but lucky for us it was where he wanted to be. We talked for a while, easily falling back into rhythm with each other like we saw each other every day. Too soon Jamey had to head back to the kitchen and Kendrick moved down the bar to fill a drink order. While we'd been catching up the place had filled up quite a bit. It was a Friday, so it would get packed. It was always good to see the place was bringing in a solid crowd.

As I looked around checking out the crowd a bit, a pair of familiar brown eyes caught mine. It was Mia, just walking through the door with a girl with lots of blonde hair, lots of curves, and a bright smile on her face. Mia, on the other hand, looked...resigned, maybe? Like she was there because she had to be, not necessarily because she wanted to be. As our eyes met, hers lit up and she smiled at me. The idea that I was the one who had put that smile on her face, that she was glad to see me, made my chest feel warm. I felt myself smiling back at her across the bar. She looked fucking amazing. Her light golden-brown hair was down, the shiny curls and waves laying over her shoulders. Her eyes looked a little darker than usual, her lips a soft pink, and I realized with a little surprise that I'd never seen her with makeup on. Mia's friend grabbed her hand and started to pull her across the pub toward a group of people in the far corner from where I sat. Mia looked in their direction for a second, then looked back at me, shrugged, and gave me a little wave. She and her friend were obviously meeting a group, so my momentary thought that I might get to spend some time with her wasn't likely. I was disappointed but I wouldn't impose myself on her time with her friends. At least I could still see her from where I was sitting.

"Hot blonde, huh?" Cal's voice startled me out of my thoughts. I'd completely forgotten that he was sitting there next to me.

"What?" He was talking about Mia's friend, right? I hadn't noticed much about her.

"The blonde you were staring at. The one with all the curves?"

"I wasn't staring at the blonde. The girl she's with is my neighbor. I've never seen her in here before."

"The tall girl, that's your neighbor?"

I nodded as Cal checked Mia out. She was taking off her coat and her snug long sleeve black top and jeans fit her lean body to perfection.

"Yeah, she's hot in her own way, I guess. I can see it." He took a sip of his whiskey and nodded more as he went on. "Yeah, I get it. No tits to speak of but those long legs and that ass...nice."

I reached out and smacked Cal on the back of the head.

"Stop talking about her like she's a pile of body parts. She's a nice girl." Besides, her tits looked great in that top. More wasn't always better.

Cal turned to me with a knowing look in his eyes.

"Oh, it's like that, is it?

"No, it's not like anything." I wasn't getting pulled into this with him. Cal was like a dog with a bone if he got wind of something he could tease you about.

Luckily Kendrick walked over just then and started up a discussion about some new trade prospect for the local baseball team. I'd watch just about any sport, but I didn't care much about trade rumors. I had something else taking my attention right then, anyway.

As Kendrick, Cal, and a couple guys down the bar next to him debated pros and cons of various trade possibilities, I watched as one of the guys in Mia's group shifted closer to her. He was about the same height as Mia and he was talking to her, getting close, probably using the fact that it was loud to lean in. He was wearing a sweater that looked expensive and his hair was styled. I could see his perfect white teeth all the way across the pub as he smiled at Mia. A pinky ring shone on his hand as he lifted his drink to take a sip. Who the hell wore a pinky ring?

Mia's head was bent and she was fiddling with the beer bottle sitting on the table next to her. I liked that she was apparently drinking beer, not some frou-frou drink. She didn't strike me as the frou-frou drink type. She looked shy like she had when we first talked. She didn't act that way around me anymore unless she was unsure of something. She sure hadn't been shy when she had demanded to finish my massage or teased me out of my shit mood.

The smile that thought brought to my face died as the douche put his hand on her arm. Mia visibly tensed and I tensed up along with her. I wanted to cross the room and punch him in the face. Couldn't the fuckwad see that he was making her nervous? He needed to back the fuck off and move his hand now. Just as I had that thought, Mia eased her arm away from his touch, smiled politely at him and moved around the table to say something to her friend. Even after she moved away pretty boy continued to watch her. I knew I had no right to tell him to stop looking at someone who didn't belong to him, but I sure as hell wanted to. Sure, I'd been staring at Mia, too, but we were friends...sort of...or at least friendly neighbors. I wasn't some creep leering at her in a bar. She looked okay now talking with her friend and I felt myself calm down a little. I knew I had to distract myself or I was going to sit and watch her all night.

I knew a foolproof distraction. I turned to Cal.

"I haven't kicked your ass in darts in way too long, Junior. Let's go."

Mission accomplished. Cal was the most competitive guy I knew. I hated to lose my perfect view of Mia, but I followed Cal as he trash-talked his way over to the dart boards.

⌒

After soundly kicking Cal's ass several times – Cal sucked at darts, so the result was never really in doubt – we started making our way back across the pub to the bar. I split off from Cal to hit the men's room. As I made my way back to the bar, I scanned the pub for Mia as casually as I could. I saw a few of the people she had been with but didn't spot her. Figuring she must have gone on home, I turned and walked right into her.

"Oof, wow." Mia bounced off me a bit and I grabbed her shoulders to steady her. "I knew you were solid, but you're like walking into a brick wall." She laughed as she looked up me. I felt my dick stir at the feel of her shoulders under my hands and standing so close to her. She looked so pretty, her cheeks pink either from a few drinks or the warmth of the pub. Whatever the reason, it was a good look for her. I realized I'd been standing there too long just looking at her and forced myself to drop my hands. I didn't have room to step back much but that was more than okay by me.

"Hey, I was just wondering if you'd headed home yet."

"I'm going to in a few minutes, but I wanted to find you and at least say hi before I headed out." I liked the fact that she'd been looking for me, had specifically come over to talk to me, not just run into me – literally – by accident.

"Thanks, I'm glad you did." She had no idea how glad. "I haven't seen you in here before. First time?"

"I'm ashamed to say yes. I've lived down the street for two years and I've never made it in. I keep saying I'm going to get out more but somehow it never happens. My friend, Meg, dragged me along tonight to meet up with some of her co-workers. I'm glad she did, though. I like it."

"I'll tell my friends you said that. Two of them own the pub and another runs the kitchen." I hoped I didn't sound like I was bragging. I wasn't trying to, just letting her know that her appreciation for the pub would be passed along.

"Really? That's amazing that they're friends of yours. I'll definitely be back." She took another look around the pub like she was taking it in, then looked up at me. "Speaking of your friends, I don't want to keep you. I just wanted to say a quick hi. I'm going to find Meg and see if I can convince her to head out."

"Hey, I was going to leave soon, too. If you're going now, I'll just go with you. We can walk it together and you can leave Meg to her fun if she's not ready to go." If I had a chance to spend a little time with Mia tonight, I was going to take it. Walking back to the complex together was the perfect opportunity.

"I can say for sure that Meg's not ready to go. She never is," Mia said with a smile. It didn't sound like a criticism, just a fact. "She'd leave for me if I wanted to go, but she'll be more than happy to stay since I can walk back with you. I just need to tell her, and we can go. Do you need to let your friends know?"

I looked over at the bar, caught Kendrick's eye, and pointed to the door to let him know I was taking off. He eyed Mia standing next to me and gave me a big smile and a thumbs up. I knew I'd get shit later for leaving with her, but right then I didn't care.

I turned back to Mia. "Done. Let's find Meg and let her know."

I followed Mia to a high-top table where the blonde I'd seen her come in with sat with a few others from their group. The pretty boy who'd been talking with Mia earlier stood nearby. Mia's friend looked first at her then up at me for a second as I stopped behind Mia.

"Meg, this is my neighbor, Dante." Mia looked over her shoulder at me with a smile. "Dante, this is my best friend, Meg."

Meg eyed me and I felt sure that I would have received a full head to toe appraisal if Mia hadn't been standing in front of me blocking Meg's view.

"So, this is Dante. It's good to meet you." Meg's smile was friendly, but there was something in it that said she wasn't 100% sold on me just yet.

"You, as well, Meg." I might not dress like her co-workers and I wouldn't be caught dead wearing a pinky ring, but I could do "polite and friendly" with the best of them when I needed to.

Mia brought Meg's attention back to her. "Hey, I was talking a minute with Dante and he's ready to head home, so I'm just going to walk back with him. I know you'd go if I wanted you to but there's really no reason when I can walk back with Dante."

Meg looked at me again and I swore I could see a little mischief in her eyes. "Hmm, and we're sure Dante here can be trusted to walk you home?" She'd asked the question to Mia, but she was looking at me as she spoke. The way she said it – "walk you home" – made it sound like I was escorting Mia home from a high school dance. For some reason, it made me smile.

"Yes, ma'am, I promise to see Mia home safely."

I could see that Meg's question had Mia a little flustered. It was cute.

"Don't be ridiculous. He's not walking me home, just…walking with me as we both go home to our apartment complex. He's my neighbor, of course he can be trusted. It's not like he's some random guy I just met in a bar."

Mr. Douchebag walked over to stand next to Meg. He had obviously overheard – or been listening in on – the conversation.

"Mia, you don't need to walk all that way. If Meg's not ready to go, I'd be happy to drive you home. My car's in the valet lot. They'll bring it right to the door for us. Just let me get my coat and we can go."

I kept my posture relaxed as I eyed him. He was several inches shorter than me and looked like he kept himself in okay shape. I wanted to puff up a bit and give him the stare-down, but I held back. I had the feeling that Meg was watching closely to see how I would react to him. I let myself shift a tiny bit closer to Mia and the look on Meg's face said she had noted even that small move.

"Thank you, Mike, that's very nice of you, but it's really not far. I'm fine walking with Dante." Mia smiled politely and started to turn to Meg. Mr. Douchebag frowned. He obviously wasn't going to let it go that easily.

"I don't know Mia. It's gotten colder since we've been here and it might feel like a longer walk than you think. You shouldn't be out in the cold. I can give you a ride. The Mercedes even has seat warmers." He smiled his perfect white smile.

Yeah, I bet he wanted to give her a ride and it wasn't in his fancy car. Meg was starting to look irritated with her co-worker and even Mia's politeness seemed to be slipping a little. "I appreciate it but really, I'm fine. Thank you." She turned to give Meg a quick hug. "Talk to you tomorrow. Text me when you get home."

Meg returned the hug. "Same with you, Meems. Night, Dante."

"Night, Meg." I didn't say anything to Mr. Douchebag, just let my eyes connect with his for a second. He looked like he was pissed, but trying not to show it. The fact that Mia was leaving with me was not making him happy. Too bad for him.

I slid my eyes away from his and smiled down at Mia. "Ready?"

"Yep, let's go." Mia led the way to the door, stopping for a second when we reached it to slip on her coat. I held it for her while she slipped her arms into it. She pulled her long hair from the collar, zipped it up, and stepped out of the pub with me behind her.

Chapter 9

Mia

*M*ike was right, it had gotten colder while we were in the pub. I pulled my coat a little closer, but the cold air felt good after the heat and closeness of the pub. And I'd rather be walking home next to Dante than getting a ride of any kind from Mike.

I glanced over at Dante as we walked and noticed that although he'd slipped his hands in his pockets, he was strolling along with no coat on. The long sleeve t-shirt he had on hugged his biceps and chest. It looked good but it didn't look warm. "You're not even cold, are you?" It was obvious he wasn't, but the question popped out anyway.

"No." Dante shrugged. "I actually think it feels good out here."

"I agree, but I'd be freezing my ass off if I didn't have a coat on."

"That would be a damn shame," Dante grinned and shot me a side-eye look. "If your fine ass was gone, I mean."

What the...did Dante just flirt with me? Before I could even process the thought, he went on.

"I'm always warm and I hate wearing a coat. They're never comfortable and I usually don't need one. If you see me wearing a coat you'll know to stay inside because it's too cold for a fragile thing like you to be out," he teased.

"Fragile, yeah, that's me." At 5'9' the last thing I was, was delicate or fragile. "Normal is more like it. Must be nice, though, not to get cold." I grumbled.

"Yeah, saves on heating bills, for sure." Dante said as he grinned again.

A mental image of Dante walking around his apartment shirtless with only shorts, or even less, on rose up in front of me and almost stopped me in my tracks. Dante noticed the hesitation in my step and stopped for a second, looking at me with an eyebrow raised in question. I just shook my head and kept walking. Dante fell into step beside me again.

"And no need to pay extra for seat warmers in the truck, either," he joked with just a bit of sarcasm.

So now I was thinking about Dante's butt and how well he filled out the jeans he was wearing. Aaaand now I was blushing. Dammit. This crush I had on Dante was getting out of control. I looked down and hoped my hair covered my burning cheeks.

"No, I guess there wouldn't be."

I felt Dante's gaze for a second and when he next spoke his tone had changed.

"So, the seat warmer guy, Mike, I think you called him. He someone you're interested in? He seems pretty interested in you."

I was surprised at the question. That was kind of random. Dante's voice was tight, like he was a little irritated, maybe? Could he tell I'd been thinking about him as way more than a neighbor or friend? Was he annoyed with me and trying to change the subject?

I looked over at him, but he was looking straight ahead now, not meeting my eyes. What had he asked me? Was I interested in Mike? "No. I...not really."

"No or not really? He seems like he has a lot going for him. Nice clothes, nice car apparently."

This was weird. Did Dante *want* me to say I was interested in Mike? He hadn't even spoken a word to him in the pub that I could remember. Why would he care either way? I looked over at Dante again, but he was still staring straight ahead as we walked. He seemed tense now. Was he wishing he'd stayed at the pub with his friends? Why were we talking about some guy I'd only met twice?

"I guess, but...I don't know. He's nice enough. He's attractive." Dante made a low noise that sounded like a grunt but didn't say anything, so I went on. "I don't know, there's just nothing there if that makes sense. I don't have any interest in knowing more about him." Not like I did about Dante. Him, I wanted to know every last detail. "I don't want to spend the time or energy. And ugh, even hearing myself say that out loud makes me feel like a terrible person. Yuck. Like I'm so special and he's not worth my time."

"You're not a terrible person, Mia. You know that." Dante sounded a little more relaxed now and when I looked at him, he met my eyes. There was something there I hadn't seen before, a look I couldn't quite decipher. And if I kept looking at Dante as I walked, I was going it walk into a light post. Wouldn't that be just what I needed right now?

I looked forward again. "No, I know. I'm not terrible but really, everyone is worth the time and energy to get to know them."

"You're right, but I know what you mean. Some people we're drawn to. We think about them when we're not with them, wonder what they're doing or thinking. Want to be around them." Dante's voice was a little rougher now. He was obviously thinking about someone specific. I wondered who the lucky girl was.

"Yes, exactly. And for me at least, Mike...that's not him."

We had reached our apartment complex and I started up the steps in front of Dante. I got the strangest feeling that he was staring at my butt as we climbed. And that's called wishful thinking, I told myself. We reached our floor and I turned to face Dante, just to see him making a beeline for his door.

"Hey, thanks for walking home with me," I said to his back as he walked away from me. I felt a twinge at the thought of how eager he seemed to be away from me.

He stopped and turned, his hand resting on his doorknob. He looked at me with kind of a half-smile, that unfamiliar look from before still lingering in his eyes. "Thank you, too. Night, Mia." Dante slipped in his door and closed it quietly behind him.

Okay then. I stood staring at Dante's door. The whole walk had been kind of weird with an undercurrent I couldn't figure out. Finally, I noticed the cold again and shrugged. I wasn't going to figure anything out by standing out here and freezing. Not to mention what Dante might think if he looked out and saw me standing here staring at his door. I unlocked my door and walked inside. Whatever had happened, this strange night was over. After texting Meg that I was home safe and receiving a thumbs up and kissy face emoji in return, I headed for bed and the inevitable dreams of Dante.

Chapter 10

Dante

I headed to the gym earlier than usual on Saturday. I'd slept like shit, my dreams full of Mia smiling her sweet smile at me as she turned away and walked into the arms of that douchebag from the pub last night. When I'd joked about those stupid seat warmers he was so proud of and she'd started blushing like a school girl with a crush, I'd wanted to punch something. Preferably pretty boy's face. I was sure it was a sign that she was into him and being shy about it. When she said she wasn't, that he wasn't for her, my chest had filled with stupid hope. I'd calmed down in one way, but revved up in another. It was dumb, I knew it. Just because she wasn't into him didn't mean she was into me. Sure, I'd caught her looking once or twice when I had my shirt off around her, but that didn't mean anything. I didn't think she was around that many shirtless guys, that could easily just be her noticing me because I was the only one there. I told myself that but my brain, and let's be honest, my dick, were stuck on the thought that if she wasn't interested in Mike, the door was still open for her to be interested in me. She hadn't mentioned being into anyone else, right? Maybe she wasn't thinking about me that way just yet, but could she? Was it a remote possibility? When we'd gotten back to the complex and I had a perfect view of her nice, tight ass all the way up the steps, it had been all I could do to keep from grabbing it, grabbing her. I'd practically run for my apartment to keep myself from jumping her or blurting out something stupid. My brain had been going in circles, still was. I was going to drive myself crazy with this shit. Which brought me back to the crappy night of no sleep and the earlier-than-usual start at the gym.

Thankfully, Saturdays were our busiest day at the gym, so I had plenty to keep me occupied. I did my own workout, ran a couple youth classes, trained some individual clients, cleaned and restocked equipment and sparred with one of Dev's better fighters. He wasn't as big as he needed to be yet, but he was fast. We weren't going all out, mostly working on technique and strategy, but he gave me a good fight. As I headed home for the day, I was physically tired but felt good. Kendrick and Cal were spending the evening with their parents and Jamey was working as usual. My plan was to grab dinner, chill, and hopefully get a decent night's sleep without my sweet neighbor filling my mind.

I woke up on Sunday feeling more settled than I had in a while. At some point the night before, I'd decided I was going to feel Mia out on how she saw me, maybe put myself out there a little and see if she responded. I didn't usually need to be subtle with women. I wasn't a caveman, but I was usually pretty direct. Hell, most of the time women came on to me. But Mia was different, and she was going to need a different approach. I'd flirted with her a little, but minor stuff, mostly slips that happened when I wasn't thinking. Like my comments about her ass Friday night and then staring at it as we went up the stairs. Mia didn't seem to catch it, though. Maybe I needed to be just a little more obvious and see how she responded. If she seemed into it, into me, then it was on. I knew two things: I liked being around Mia and I was getting more desperate every day to be inside her. Other than that, I wasn't sure where I wanted this to go but if she was in, we could figure it out together.

A few hours later, I was feeling desperate for Mia in a whole different way. You know that saying that if anything can go wrong, it will, or the one about best laid plans being sure to go sideways? By Sunday night I wasn't thinking anymore about how to ease into a relationship with Mia. I was pacing my floor wracking my brain for a way to get her to help me keep my shit locked down without sounding like a lunatic.

I'd spent the day around the apartment doing laundry, dishes, vacuuming – all the shit you've gotta do if you don't have a maid and don't want to live in a dump. Then I'd spent a few hours at Kendrick's, just hanging out with him, Cal, and Jamey. Cal was headed back out of town soon and it was good to have time with all of us there. As expected, I got shit from the guys for leaving the pub with Mia a couple nights before, but they let it rest faster than I expected. I dropped Jamey at his apartment on the way home and all was good. That was, until I hit the parking lot at my complex. As I pulled into my spot in the back corner, I noticed a sliver car with tinted windows parked across the lot. It hit me that it was probably the same car that Mrs. Curr had bitched at Mia about. As I got out of my truck, I realized that although the silver car was parked with its lights off, it was running. By itself that wasn't a big deal, they could just be waiting for somebody in one of the apartments. But the feeling of being watched was back, too. I felt the hair stand up on the back of my neck and along my arms. I wished I could see into the car, even just to see how many people were inside, but the dark windows and dark night made it impossible. As I stood there deciding whether to approach the car, whoever was inside made the decision for me. They shifted into drive and drove quickly out of the lot, leaving me still standing by my truck watching them. There was really nothing about the whole situation that should be making me uneasy, but something just felt off. As I headed to my apartment, I felt my phone buzz in my pocket. I pulled it out, saw Dev's name and answered. That's when my night really went to shit.

Dev had the unpleasant task of giving me the news that my fucking ex and her fucking boyfriend were going to be at the annual sponsor event in downtown the following Saturday. It was one of our biggest events of the year and was usually a good time. All the sponsors involved with the state and regional boxing association would be there schmoozing with each other and the boxers and gyms they sponsored. Even though Dev and I didn't compete anymore we were well-known and well-liked. The event was a great opportunity to secure sponsors to support the expansion of our youth boxing program. We had big plans and needed big money to pull them off. There would be other opportunities, but none as big or as important as this event. And now I had to deal with the fact that Justin and Haven would be in my face the whole night, no doubt stirring the pot to see if they could get me to squirm. Justin on his own would trash talk some and be an ass but he would eventually back off. He had his own sponsors to keep happy and starting shit at the annual event wasn't the way to do that. Haven, on the other hand, was a bitch down to her core. Get a few of the event's free-flowing drinks in her and who knew what kind of chaos she would cause.

"You'll just have to handle it," Dev said as I held my phone so tightly I was afraid the case might crack. "Haven will be a train wreck, no doubt, but we need to look like we're credible business owners who are a good bet for sponsors. Getting into it with Haven or Justin at the event could ruin a big opportunity. A lot of these people know us, but as fighters, not business owners. We need to make a good impression."

"I know," I groaned into the phone. I'd put it on speaker and set it on my couch. I sat next to it, leaned forward with my elbows on my knees, my head in my hands. "Believe me, I know that. I don't know why or how Haven can push my buttons so easy, but she can. And just seeing Justin has always made me want to punch that smirk off his face."

"You and me both, brother. He has some talent as a fighter but as a human being he sucks. You know they'll try to start something just for the fun of seeing if they can make you lose your shit. Just go in prepared and you'll keep your head. I'll ask Nic if you can borrow some of her Zen crystals and shit."

The humor in Dev's voice didn't improve my mood any. Dev's girlfriend, Nicole, was into crystals and Zen gardens and all kinds of other woo-woo crap. He was joking about it now, but his refusal to take it seriously was putting a real strain on their relationship.

"Fuck you, Dev. I don't need Zen crystals, whatever the hell those are."

"Fair enough. Figure out what you do need and do it before Saturday. You need to be a calm, cool, fucking charming professional at this event, not a hot-headed street brawler who can't deal with your trash-talking ex and her lapdog."

Dev hung up and it took everything in me not to smash the phone on the floor. I wasn't mad at Dev, not really. Everything he said was true. Well, except the part about the Zen crystals. I didn't need those to keep my cool. With a flash of clarity, I realized what I did need. Not what, really, who. Mia. I'd thought many times over the past few weeks how calm, how settled I always felt when I was with Mia. It was a weird contrast to the fact that my dick was usually hard as diamond at the same time. Her touch, her scent, the sound of her voice, just being near her – they all seemed to center me. I realized that sounded kind of crazy. Not as woo-woo as Nicole's crystals maybe, but still out there.

The thing was, though, it was true. I remembered how good it had felt with her standing beside me when Mrs. Curr had been giving me shit about my parking. That had been a minor thing, but still just having her there had made all the difference.

So all I had to do was convince Mia to go to the event with me. Having her there would help me stay calm, help me keep my head clear and my shit locked down. I needed her to go as my date, though, not as my friend. Having her there as "just a friend" would just give Haven and Justin more ammunition to jab at me with. But how was I going to ask Mia to be my date when I didn't even know yet if she was interested in me? What if I spooked her and she turned me down? I didn't have time for the whole "put your best game out there and see how it goes" approach that I had planned. This was Sunday night. The event was Saturday. Fuck, Mia sometimes worked on Saturdays if she was covering for someone. What if she was scheduled to work? I needed to ask her as soon as I could in case she needed to switch or ask off. Maybe...maybe I could ask her if she would go and pretend to be my date, pretend that she was there as more than a friend. That could work. Okay, it was basically asking her to lie, that part wasn't great, but Mia had a big heart. She'd do it to help me out and I wouldn't blow it and send her running in the opposite direction if she wasn't into me just yet. I couldn't ask her for real and take the chance that would happen. I couldn't do this event without her. I had to have her with me.

I looked at the clock. It wasn't that late and Mia should be home. If I waited until tomorrow, I had no idea when I would see her. With her work schedule and mine we would often go days without even seeing each other in passing. I had to go ask her now.

Chapter 11

Mia

When I opened my door and saw Dante standing there my heart jumped a little and I smiled at him. I hadn't seen him since we walked home from the pub together and I missed him, as strange as that sounded. It wasn't like we were dating or anything, but it was always a better day when even a few minutes of it included Dante.

The smile fell from my face as I let Dante into my apartment and realized how agitated he was. He was pacing back and forth, running his hand over his head and down his face.

"Dante, what's going on?"

I wasn't prepared for the flood of words that came spilling out. I'd never seen Dante like this and between my concern for him and the fact that something was obviously very wrong, my mind was swirling and I was having trouble following.

There was a big event...Saturday downtown...important sponsors... his ex would stir shit...he needed to stay in control...would I go...but wait, *pretend to* be his date? What? Not a real date? But he wanted me to go? To this super important thing. With lots of important people.

Wow.

An important event with important people. Kind of my worst nightmare.

I knew I was standing there staring at Dante. He kept glancing at me as he talked, sounding more and more tense as he did. I could feel how wide my eyes were and I wasn't sure I was breathing. Could I do what Dante was asking? Pretend to be his date at this big event? For him, could I do it?

Dante stopped suddenly and I could feel the tension I'd heard in his voice radiating off his body in waves.

His jaw was clenched. "You know what? It was a stupid idea. I'll leave you alone." He turned abruptly toward the door.

Wait…he was leaving? I'd barely even caught up to what he'd been saying.

"Dante, wait. Don't leave."

I put my hand on his arm and his muscles there were so rigid it seemed like they might shatter. It seemed like he might shatter. "I'm just…I'm trying to catch up."

Dante shook his head at my words, but he turned away from the door. My hand fell from his arm and I stepped back a little but stayed close. It still felt like he was on the brink of walking out.

"Let's just forget it, okay? Of course you don't want to go and pretend to be with me. I'm sorry, I shouldn't have asked. "

"Dante, stop. You should have asked. I'm just trying to catch up. This event is important, and you want an ally with you. I can understand that." Well, based on the bits and pieces I'd caught I thought I kind of understood. The event part anyway. The "pretend to be with him" part? Yeah, I had to skip over that for right now.

"That's not what I'm worried about. It's just…" I took a deep breath and wrapped my arms over my stomach, willing myself to push through my embarrassment. "It's just that I suck in situations like that."

Dante finally met my eyes. The lack of judgment in them helped me go on. "This sounds really big and really, really important to you. To someone who's super shy like me…" I swallowed hard. "Let's just say I don't typically shine."

Dante nodded as I talked, showing me he understood. His shoulders slumped. "I get that. I do. I didn't even consider that. I'm a huge asshole and only thought about how much it would help me to have you there. I forget how shy you are because you don't act that way most of the time around me anymore. I can see why it would be hard for you. Let's just forget it, okay?"

"Stop." I told him again. "You are not an asshole."

He was right, though. I wasn't shy with him at all. Could this maybe work? I really wanted to do this for him. I was surprised how much. I couldn't stand the thought of him facing a tough situation alone when I could help. Be brave, girl, I told myself. Push yourself out there.

I took a deep breath and took the leap. "I want to do it, Dante."

Dante's eyes lit up with cautious hope and surprise at my words and I could see him relax a tiny bit.

"I want to help but Dante, I'm worried I'm going to embarrass you. I don't want to freeze up or get tongue-tied and make you look bad."

"You could never embarrass me or make me look bad." Dante was definitely more relaxed, but I could still see concern in his eyes and hear it in his voice. "How about this? I promise I won't leave you on your own or call a lot of attention to you. But I don't want to force you into it, Mia. I couldn't live with myself if I put you through something that scared you."

As he talked, I realized that the concern Dante was feeling was for me, not about me. He wasn't at all worried that I would make him look bad, although I still wasn't so sure. He was worried that he was asking me to do something that was too hard for me. And that made me want to do it even more.

"I'll do it. I want to do it." I blurted out before I could talk myself out of it. "If you promise me you won't leave me alone or make me give a speech or anything, I'll go."

Dante smiled, his full, gorgeous, breathtaking smile this time. "Got it. No ditching you. And the big speech I had planned for you is off the table."

We both laughed as Dante held out his hand to shake mine. "We have a deal." He held on to my hand a second longer as our eyes met. "Thank you," he said sincerely.

"You're very welcome." My heart swelled with the evidence that agreeing to go to the event with Dante had made him so happy and relieved. It was hard to believe it had such an impact, but it obviously did. The fact that it was a "pretend" date and not a real one made my heart twinge a bit, but hey at least he wanted me with him. I was sure he had a list a mile long of gorgeous women he could call if he just wanted a pretty face next to him so he wasn't solo. But he wanted a friend, someone who would be on his side. So, he only liked me as a friend. That was important, too. And if it was what I could get, I'd take it.

⌒

It hit me as I was getting ready for work on Tuesday that I had no idea what Dante did. Ok, that wasn't entirely true. I knew he worked at a gym and he used to be a competitive athlete. That was pretty much it. I'd talked his ear off about my job a couple weeks ago when I gave him his second massage, but he hadn't said anything about his job. If we were going to this event in 5 days and I was supposed to be his date, shouldn't I know something about what he did at the gym? Especially since it sounded like the event was related to whatever it was?

Dante and I had exchanged numbers Sunday night so we could be in touch about Saturday. I wondered now if I should text him and ask what he did? That seemed pretty weird. What would I say? *Yeah, about Saturday, what is it you do exactly? As your pretend date I should probably know.* Okay, maybe I shouldn't use that exact wording, but really that was the gist of it. I couldn't pretend to be with Dante without knowing more about him. If someone made a comment or asked a simple question about Dante or our supposed relationship and I had no idea how to answer, we'd both look like idiots or, even worse, liars. We had a few days. I could get a crash course in Dante 101.

I picked up my phone and tapped on Dante's number to send a text.

Me: Hi, it's Mia. I was just thinking. I don't know much about your job. This event on Saturday is related, right? I should probably know at least something.

Three dots popped up right away.

Dante: Shit, you're right. Didn't think of that. I'm a trainer and part owner of the gym I work at.

I waited to see if there was more but nothing else popped up. That was a start, but surely Dante didn't think that was enough information.

Me: Like a personal trainer?

Dante: No. Well, sort of. But more like a coach.

No, but sort of. Ookaay.

Me: And you used to compete in a sport, right?

Dante: Right.

I groaned. This was like pulling teeth. Was this top-secret information? Maybe I'd just caught him at a busy time at work.

Me: So…am I allowed to know which sport? If this is a bad time, I'll stop bugging you.

Dante: You're not bugging me. Boxing.

Boxing? I hadn't expected that. I didn't know why.

Me: You're a professional boxer?

The dots danced and stopped and danced again.

Dante: Was. Yeah.

I tried to picture Dante as a boxer, but the image just wouldn't come. To say I didn't know much about boxing was an understatement. I may have watched 30 seconds of a boxing match in the past as I flipped though coverage of the Olympics, but I definitely hadn't stopped to watch it. Did Dante train boxers at his gym? Was that what this event was about? I had more questions now than I had before. Looking back down at my phone I realized that if I didn't hurry, I was going to be late for work. I'd have to figure this out later. Maybe I could google the basics of boxing or something. Realizing I hadn't responded to Dante, I tapped out a quick message.

Me: Okay, thanks. Gotta run to work. Talk more later.

Seeing a thumbs up emoji in response from Dante, I threw my phone in my purse and headed out the door for work.

Pulling my phone out a few hours later as I took my lunch break, I noticed that I had missed a text Dante had sent earlier.

Dante: If you're not busy tonight I can fill you in more on what I do. You're right, you should know more. I should be home by eight.

Me: Sounds good. Come over when you get home?

Dante: See you tonight.

The rest of the day flew by and I knew it was because I'd be seeing Dante later. I was looking forward to learning more about Dante's life and his work at the gym. I had to keep reminding myself that this was all because of the fake date on Saturday. Dante wasn't coming over tonight because he was truly interested in me getting to know him better. He was doing it so I could convincingly play the role of his date on Saturday. But either way I'd get to spend time with Dante and I couldn't help but be happy about it.

Chapter 12

Dante

I rushed home from work, my mind full of thoughts of the evening ahead with Mia. I kept reminding myself that it wasn't a date. I was giving her the basics of my job and the sport that was so much a part of my life, all so she could pretend she was with me for real at the event on Saturday. But no matter how much I told myself that, I couldn't wait to see her and spend time with her.

I was nervous how she was going to respond to the boxing aspects of my job and my life. When it had taken her so long to text back this morning after I'd told her I used to fight professionally, I'd realized that I had no idea how she felt about boxing. Some people loved it, but a lot of others, especially women, were completely turned off by it. They just saw it as hitting another person and didn't want anything to do with it, didn't want to learn anything about it. As I'd waited for Mia's response, I'd remembered the conversation I'd had with Kenan about his girl, Jasmine, a couple weeks ago, and how she'd been disgusted with him for being a fighter. How I'd told him to think about whether she was the right girl for him if she couldn't love, or at least tolerate, something that was such a big part of him. It had made me wonder about how Mia had reacted when she'd read my text. I wished I could have seen her face. Not knowing what she was thinking was making me crazy. When she hadn't responded to my text right away,

I'd started to think the worst. When she finally did reply I couldn't tell much from her response. At least she was willing to let me come over tonight to tell her more. That had to be a good sign, right?

I knocked on Mia's door with knots still in my stomach. The next hour or so could determine whether I still had a date for Saturday. More important, though, it could determine whether Mia and I were still just friendly neighbors, or if there was the potential for some-thing more. If I was being honest, the potential for something more had been on my mind a lot lately. Depending on how she felt about boxing and fighters, that might be over. If I lost whatever it was I had with Mia now, it would be hard. But I couldn't be with someone who couldn't deal with or respect a big part of my life.

Mia answered my knock right away and opened the door with a small smile on her face.

"Hey, Dante. You got here fast."

"Yeah, I made pretty good time." Because I'd blown through the speed limit and taken the world's fastest shower. I was ready to get this over with one way or the other.

Chapter 13

Mia

*D*ante was agitated again, not nearly as bad as Sunday, but definitely wound up. Maybe he was still coming down from a tough day at work. Hopefully he'd relax a little now that he was here.

"Grab a seat wherever. I was going to get a drink. Want anything? I have water, orange juice, white wine, and beer." I'd actually stopped on the way home to get the beer I knew he drank, but he didn't need to know that. When he asked for one, I was glad I'd made the effort.

I walked back into the living room, Dante's beer and my wine in hand. Dante had chosen to sit on one end of my couch, so I handed him his beer and sat down on the other end. For a second, I felt a little awkward – should I have sat in the chair catty-corner to the couch instead? But we were going need to be a lot closer on Saturday night than we were now if anyone was to believe we were dating. Might as well get used to a little close proximity right now. Anyway, we'd been a lot closer when I gave Dante his massages and when we were talking in the pub. Sitting one cushion away from him was nothing, right? Right.

I cleared my throat.

"So you're a boxer, huh?"

"Was. Am. Yeah." Dante took a sip of his beer. "Does that bother you?" The intense look he gave me as he asked that threw me a little bit.

"Bother me? No. Why would it bother me?" I knew my confusion was clear.

"Some people really don't like boxing. They don't understand it, are almost offended by it. They kind of look down on the whole sport, including the fighters."

"Really? Well, I guess…it does seem pretty violent. I guess I can see where people might be bothered by that. I just haven't ever watched it. I don't have any idea how it works other than the obvious."

"What's the obvious?" Dante seemed less stressed now, but his eyes and voice were still tense.

"Oh, well the ring and the gloves and the bell and all that. And the fighters hit each other, of course. If you knock the other guy out, you win." I shrugged as I looked back at Dante. "Other than that, I don't have a clue."

Dante nodded. "The best way to learn more is to watch a couple fights. I can walk you through what's going on."

"That sounds good. Let's do that. But is there a fight we can watch tonight?"

Dante grinned as he set his beer aside. "There's always one you can watch if you know where to find it. Grab your laptop."

I jumped up to do that then rejoined Dante on the couch. We had to sit closer together so we could both see the laptop screen. I loved Dante's woodsy scent and had to fight hard not to lean a little closer and sniff him. Or lick him. Our closeness didn't seem to phase Dante. He perched my laptop on the muscular leg closest to me, clicked a few buttons, and brought up a video of a fight.

Dante started by explaining the basics of what happened behind the scenes before the fight starts, the weigh-in, all of the prep, how fighters might warm-up and focus. Then he started the video of the fight and turned the volume down. He explained what was happening, why a fighter threw a certain punch or moved a certain way, when one scored a point and what that meant. How a fight could be won by knockout or decision or end in a draw. I didn't love watching the two fighters hit each other, especially when one's eye got cut and started to bleed – yuck – but it was amazing to see the details Dante saw. I kept my eyes on the screen so I could follow everything, but it felt like Dante watched me as much as he watched the fight. Maybe he was checking to see if I was confused? I asked a couple of questions, but for the most part I just let him talk.

We watched two fights, then Dante clicked off the videos and turned to me.

"Make more sense now?"

"Some, yeah. There's so much going on. I didn't even catch everything you told me. I never would have known what to look for."

"There's always a lot that happens during a fight. I think it's easier to see when you've been in the middle of it." Dante had set my laptop on the floor and was leaned back a bit into the couch. He was much more relaxed than he had been.

"Do you have any of your fights we can watch?" As I asked the question a sudden wave of shyness hit me. For some reason it felt like I was asking Dante to share something really personal with me, to show me part of him others hadn't seen. That was ridiculous, I knew. His fights had been public. But I still couldn't bring myself to meet his eyes.

"You want to watch one of my fights?" Dante sounded a little surprised, a little...pleased.

"I do." I risked a peek at him while I fiddled with a loose thread on the couch. "If it's okay with you. You said that each fighter has their own style, their own signatures. I just...I feel like maybe I should see you fight at least once if I'm going to pretend to be involved with you."

A little of the light went out of Dante's eyes. "Right, that. You probably should. We can do that."

Since it was getting a little late, we agreed to get together later in the week to watch Dante's fight. As he left my apartment, Dante stopped and turned to look at me. He seemed like he wanted to say something, but he just studied me like he was looking for the answer to a question. I didn't say anything either, just raised my eyebrows in question. He shook his head, looked down at the ground, and bumped his loose fist against the door jamb a couple of times, still not speaking. Finally, he looked up into my eyes.

"Sleep well, Mia. Sweet dreams." It seemed like he was saying more than his words, but I couldn't figure out what it might be.

"Goodnight, Dante. See you in a couple days if not before."

Dante continued to study me for a few seconds, then nodded and turned to his door. I shut my door quietly and leaned against it. It was a strange ending to what had been an enjoyable but oddly intense evening. What had Dante been looking for as he studied me? Maybe I'd ask if I ever got the nerve.

Chapter 14

Dante

*I*t was Friday evening before Mia and I were able to get together again. We were both so busy at work that I hadn't seen any sign of Mia except her car in three days. It was too long. I was ready for a Mia fix. When I'd left Mia's apartment the other night, I'd just barely stopped myself from getting way too serious on her and probably blowing everything. She'd completely blown my mind by asking to watch one of my fights. Granted, it was only to make her feel more confident for our pretend date tomorrow night, but I'd already walked her through a couple fights, talked her through the basics. The fact that she specifically wanted to watch me fight... my chest swelled up again as I thought about it. It had been enough that she admitted she didn't know much...anything really...about boxing and was willing to learn more, to give it a chance. She hadn't seemed to love it, but she had watched, paid attention and asked good questions. I could hardly take my eyes off her as she watched the fights. I wanted to see how she was reacting, what she was thinking. Keeping my hands off her after she asked to watch one of my fights was hard as fuck. As I left her apartment, I wanted to thank her. Thank her for giving boxing a chance, for looking past the obvious, as she had called it, and seeing more. It felt like she was giving me a chance, seeing past just the obvious in me. It was dumb, I know, but that didn't change how it felt. I'd wanted to push her up against the door, take her mouth, and taste the sweetness that I'd been craving for weeks now. I'd managed to restrain myself, but just barely.

As I heard the knock on my door, I let out a soft groan. I wanted nothing more than to spend time with Mia, but it was going to be another evening full of self-restraint.

I'd barely opened the door and Mia hurried past me into my apartment.

"Wow, it got cold!" She kicked her shoes off right by the front door like she did in her apartment and shrugged out of her coat. She was wearing a soft pink long sleeve t-shirt, black yoga pants that fit her ass to perfection, and fuzzy gray socks. "It's starting to rain, too. Yuck." Her wrinkled up nose told me all I needed to know about what she thought of the weather. It was damn cute. As I turned to hang her coat on the rack by the door, the rain started to hit the roof and windows.

"Glad you got over here before it really let loose."

"Me, too."

Mia eyed the t-shirt and shorts I was wearing, then looked down to shake her head at my bare feet.

"It's like 40 degrees outside and you're dressed like you're at the beach."

"Ah, but I'm not outside, am I? I'm in my nice warm apartment."

"Still, it's crazy that you're not cold."

Mia turned to look around my apartment and I took the opportunity to look at her. Her hair was loose and she had no make-up on. She was beautiful, as always. And she was talking. I tuned back in. She was talking about my apartment. I hadn't thought about it, but it was the first time she'd been inside.

"It fits you. I like it." She eyed my dark brown leather couch that I'd had for a while. It was perfectly broken in and plenty big enough for a guy my size. Dev had offered to buy it from me when I'd moved out of his place, but I'd just laughed at him. No way in hell I was giving up this couch. On the wall across from the couch was my other prize possession, my huge TV. I was a stereotypical guy when it came to the fact that I considered a comfortable couch and big TV to be basic necessities for survival.

"Go ahead and crash on the couch." I chuckled as Mia plopped down quickly as if I might take back the invitation. "I'll grab us drinks. I've already got one of my fights cued up on the computer. I just need to switch it to show on the TV."

When I came back in the room with our drinks Mia was sprawled over one end of the couch. She looked like she'd found her new favorite place. She craned her neck to look at me over the back of the couch.

"You have a problem," she told me as she ran her hands over the leather of the couch.

I was certainly going to if I didn't stop picturing those hands running all over me that same way. I swallowed hard and forced my gaze away from her hands.

"What's that?"

"I've decided I'm going to live on your couch. I may never leave it again. I'll be quiet and all, but you're going to have to figure out a way to work around me."

I laughed. This girl came up with the goofiest stuff sometimes. "It's a great couch, no denying that."

I settled on the other end and sprawled out a little myself.

"What do you say? Ready to watch a fight?" I sat my drink down and picked up the remote to transfer the video to the TV screen.

"I am, but...can I ask you a question first?" Mia sat up, pulling her feet up onto the couch and angling her body toward me.

At Mia's question, I stopped fiddling with the remote and looked at her. "Sure. What do you want to know?"

Mia reached up and began twisting her hair around her finger. "How did you get interested in boxing?"

I sat back and let out a breath. "You sure you want to hear all that?"

She nodded. "I do, yes. If you don't mind telling me." I could tell by the look in her pretty brown eyes that she meant it.

"I'll try to do the short version. I have a sister who's a few years younger. She started playing volleyball when she was about 8. I had to tag along with her and my mom to her games and practices because my dad worked afternoons and weekends and I was still too young to stay by myself. The Y where my sister's team practiced had a boxing program and I used to watch them go at it. I was too young for that program, but my mom saw how fascinated I was. She saw a flyer at the grocery about beginner youth boxing at a gym nearby and signed me up. The gym was owned by Dev's uncle. That's how I got into boxing and got to know Dev. It's the only gym I've ever trained at and it's the gym where I work now. I bought in as a partner about a year ago, but Dev is still the boss."

"So, you've known Dev since you were little then. Did he box, too?" Mia was completely focused on me, her head tilted a little to the side as she put the pieces together.

"He did, yeah. He's a few years older than me and was in a different weight class so we never competed against each other. I've known him for about 20 years."

"And he owns the gym now, well... and you, too, of course." Mia gave me a little smile as she threw me that bone. I couldn't help but smile back. "Did Dev's uncle retire?"

I shook my head. "No, he passed away a few years ago. Just didn't wake up one morning. It was tough." The shock and sadness had faded over time, but some days it was still hard to believe he was gone. "Ray was a great trainer and even better man. He practically raised Dev. Hell, he practically raised all the fighters who trained in his gym. When he died Dev retired from competition and took over the gym."

Mia looked at me, her brown eyes soft with understanding. "You miss him."

"Every damn day. But Dev's making him proud, running a good place. Ray would love the youth program we've got going. He loved working with the beginners, giving them a solid grounding in the basics." I met Mia's eyes, hoping she would understand. "That's a big reason this event tomorrow night is so important. If we can get a couple sponsors interested in the youth program, we can expand it, do things the way they should be done. If I end up losing my shit because I get pushed too far, I could blow that."

I saw the determination in Mia's expression as she nodded. "Well then, we'll make sure that doesn't happen. You'll have a firm hold on all of your shit." Her head tilted again, and I waited...

"Can I ask one more question before we watch your fight?"

I couldn't help but tease her a bit. "For a shy girl you sure ask a lot of questions."

My teasing backfired as Mia stuck her tongue out at me and my dick stirred to attention. If she kept that up, she was going to find herself on her back with me sucking on that little pink tongue.

Mia went on with her question, oblivious to the fact that I was now hard for her. Maybe basketball shorts hadn't been the best choice for me to wear tonight. I shifted my position on the couch to try to make my hard-on less obvious.

"Why are you so sure that your ex and her boyfriend are going to try to cause problems?"

Now there was a subject guaranteed to make my dick deflate. Problem solved.

"Because they're shit stirrers. It's their nature. They both love to be the center of attention; they crave the spotlight. They've been in Vegas for almost a year working on some deal for a reality show that fell through. But that's their thing, to have all eyes on them. And if they can make somebody else look bad while they're doing it, even better."

"It's not my place to judge, but you were involved with this woman...why, again? I mean, she sounds lovely, but..." The sarcasm in Mia's voice couldn't be clearer.

I dropped my head back on the couch in defeat. Yes, my ex was a self-absorbed bitch, yet I'd been with her for almost 2 years. I rolled my head toward Mia. "I thought you were only going to ask one more question."

Mia just continued to look at me.

I sighed. "I know, okay? It's hard to explain. Haven's been around boxing most of her life. Her dad is gone now, but he was a promoter for a long time, so she knows the boxing world. She was with another fighter before me. When he kind of faded out, she latched on to me." At Mia's raised eyebrows, I admitted, "Okay, it's not like I fought her on it. She just inserted herself into my life and I let her. She loved boxing, she loved to fu...um." I looked away from Mia and ran my hand over my face. Maybe mentioning that my ex had loved to fuck wasn't something to discuss with the girl I was currently interested in doing that with. The gleam in Mia's eye as I turned back to her made it clear that she had caught my slip. I cleared my throat and went on. "She liked to have a good time and she got a lot of attention at my fights. She wanted to be with a championship fighter, and I was on my way. It was all good." I shrugged. "At least I thought it was. After I won my title, I started to think about retiring and she started hooking up with Justin behind my back. I guess she was hedging her bets. I found out she was cheating on me, dumped her ass, and decided to retire all within a couple days. She moved on to Justin and has been with him since. I realized later that she'd taken information on my training plan and diet and started passing it onto Justin even before they hooked up. It wasn't top secret but just the thought that she stole from me and betrayed me while I trusted her still fires me up. I was an idiot to let her get anywhere near me. Lesson learned. The end."

"No, you can't stop there." Mia's hair swung in her face as she shook her head firmly at me. "First, don't think I didn't notice that you oh-so-casually mentioned that you won a title, which is amazing, but I still don't get why they hate you so much. It's not like *you* cheated on *her*."

"No, it's not that. What it comes down to is that I should have had to go through Justin to get to the title bout. He's a talented fighter and had a shot. But he got injured, so I didn't end up facing him. He's never quite gotten back to that level and both he and Haven blame it partly on me. I retired with the title. It belongs to someone else now, but Justin and Haven think if I agreed to fight Justin and lost, he would get another shot. According to them, I'm a pussy who's scared to fight Justin and retired so I don't ever have to face him. It's complete bullshit - my decision to retire had nothing to do with him. But that's the story they love to tell and they tell it whenever they can. I'm sure you'll hear it tomorrow."

I looked at Mia again and was surprised to see her look of irritation. Her eyes flashed with annoyance and her face was a little flushed. "Anyone who knows you knows that's completely stupid. There's no way that's true. I can see why that pisses you off. It pisses me off."

Seeing her so irritated on my behalf helped me see the humor in the situation. I laughed a little as I said, "Down, girl. You're supposed to be the calm one here."

Mia flopped back on the couch and huffed out a breath. "I know, I know. I'll be good tomorrow, I promise." She sat up and turned to me. "I know I've made you talk forever, and I really want to watch your fight, but there's one more thing I should probably know in case it comes up tomorrow."

"Okay, what's that?"

"Why did you decide to retire?" Mia's voice was a little cautious, like she thought it might be a touchy subject. It wasn't.

"I got two pretty serious concussions in a short time period – one during a fight and one from a bad car wreck. The doc at the hospital after the wreck told me that if I took another good shot to the head, I was risking anything from permanent memory loss to blindness to death. I was in the hospital for a couple days and it took a few weeks to recover. It gave me time to think. I'd achieved what I wanted to in boxing and I'd put everything else in my life on hold to get there. I still loved boxing, but I didn't want it to be the sole focus of my life anymore. I have the perfect balance now. Boxing is still a big part of my life, it's just not my whole life."

I looked over at Mia and her eyes shone now with something that looked like admiration. "That makes a lot of sense. Thanks for sharing that with me."

Suddenly, I was glad I had. Was really, really glad Mia had asked me the question. It had felt important to share it with her and I knew, even as I said it, that she would understand. This girl just seemed to get me.

Along with that feeling came the need to have her see me in action in the ring. If we were eventually going to take this anywhere beyond neighbors and friends – and I hoped like hell we were – I needed her to see me as a fighter and know that she accepted that part of me. I didn't understand it, but I felt it in my soul.

"Ready to watch the fight?"

My voice was a little rougher than normal, but Mia didn't seem to notice. She settled in again at the other end of the couch.

"Yep, let's do it."

I got the first fight going on the TV screen, then settled back. I started talking, walking Mia through what was going on. I remembered every second of these fights and what was going on around them. I talked for a bit then stopped to watch the action for a minute. Mia had a question or two, not as many as the other night, but I figured she knew more now. I made a few more comments, talking her through the first couple rounds. I realized Mia had gone quiet and looked over to check on her. She was watching the fight, but had her feet up on the couch, knees bent, with her arms wrapped around them. Although her eyes were on the screen her head was tilted down like she didn't really want to see what she was watching. She looked uncomfortable, unhappy. My heart jumped a little at the look on her face. Had she decided she hated boxing after all?

I paused the fight and turned toward her. "Mia, you okay?"

She rested her cheek on her knees and looked at me. "I am. It's just hard to watch."

"Why? Why is it hard? You were fine the other night." I tried to keep my voice even, but I was panicking a little bit. Fuck, this could be bad.

"I was, but…I didn't know those guys. This is you. It's hard to watch you get hit. I mean, I know you're okay and all but it's different watching you. I know I'm being silly. You're obviously fine and that's what you train for, but it's just hard to watch you be hurt."

For a second, I didn't know what to say. I'd started to breathe again when I realized she was okay, but then it hit me that her unhappiness was because she cared about me, cared what was happening to me. Even if it was an old fight, even if, like she said, I was obviously fine, she didn't want me to be hurt. She might only care about me as a friend, but maybe there was something more there, too?

"You're not being silly." I knew my voice was rough, but I kept going. "That means a lot to me, Mia, really. But you're right, it's what we train for. Doesn't mean some of those hits don't hurt like a bitch." I grinned as Mia smiled. There. I liked that smile on her face much better than the unhappy look from a few minutes ago. Maybe we'd watched enough. I hated to cut my time with Mia short, but maybe we should stop while she was still smiling.

"Hey, if you don't want to watch the rest, that's cool," I offered. "Really, you've seen the basics."

"No, really, I want to watch you fight if you don't mind watching it."

I'd picked up the remote to turn the TV off but at Mia's words I sat back and looked over at her.

"Mind watching my brilliant strategy and perfect form as I kick some guy's ass? I'll never get tired of that." Mia laughed like I'd hoped and rolled her eyes at me. She reached across the space that separated us to nudge me – hard – in the shoulder.

"Yeah, speaking of asses..."

I reached out to grab her fingers as she snatched her hand back. I don't know what I planned to do, but whatever it was left my head when I felt her freezing hand in mine.

"Damn, girl, what the hell? How can anyone have hands this cold and still be alive?"

Mia tugged her hand gently, but I wasn't letting go just yet. I held on to her hand and wrapped my fingers more securely around hers. It was like holding a block of ice.

"Not all of us can be abnormally warm all of the time."

I turned and put my other hand on top of her feet. I could feel that they were cold even through her socks. "I wouldn't go throwing around the word 'abnormal' when you apparently survive without your blood circulating to your extremities." Mia huffed out a little laugh and pulled on her hand again. I let go this time and sat back on the couch. "Why didn't you tell me you were cold?"

"It's okay. I'm cold a lot. It's my own fault. I should have worn a warmer shirt. This t-shirt isn't the warmest, long sleeves or not."

I stood up from the couch and headed toward my bedroom. "I have a solution. Let's take a break for a minute. Do you want another drink while I'm up?"

"Sure."

As I came back out of my bedroom, Mia was standing next to the couch stretching her arms over her head and yawning. Her shirt had ridden up a little, revealing a slim strip of smooth, pale skin. My hands twitched with the need to touch her there. To wrap my arms around her, put my mouth on her there, and taste her skin. Once this event was over tomorrow, I was going back to my plan of trying to ease into a relationship with Mia. I wasn't going to be able to keep my hands off her much longer.

With a "heads up" I threw her the sweatshirt I was carrying and then grabbed two drinks out of the fridge. She was sitting on the couch again when I got back to it, practically swimming in my sweatshirt. She was rolling the sleeves up and the shoulder seams were practically ½ way down her upper arms.

"Sorry it's a bit big."

Mia looked up at me with a smile. "Just a bit. But that's fine. Thank you, it feels great."

And it looks great, I thought. Call me a caveman but I loved seeing my shirt on her.

I started the fight again and we watched the rest straight through, each of us making comments or Mia asking the occasional question. When it was over, I looked over at Mia to see if she wanted to watch another one and she nodded. I started the fight playing and explained a few things about the format to Mia that I hadn't told her about before. I looked over to see if she understood and noticed that she was all curled up in a ball again, hands covered in the sleeves of the sweatshirt, chin on her knees. She looked like she was trying to conserve body heat.

"Still cold?"

Mia looked away from the fight and met my eyes. "A little, but it's okay. I want to watch the rest of this." She said it like she thought I might stop the video and make her go home because she was cold.

Without thinking it through, I held my left arm out along the back of the couch toward Mia and said, "Okay, then, come here."

"Do what?" Mia's voice squeaked a bit as she asked.

"Scoot over here. Snuggle up. You're freezing, I'm practically a furnace. I'll keep you warm while we watch the rest of the fight."

"Oh...hmm. Okay." Mia slid cautiously closer to me on the coach. When she got close enough and slid under my arm, I draped it over her shoulders and across her back, then pulled her legs over my lap and draped my other arm across them. I had her completely wrapped up, cocooned in warmth.

"Good?" I tipped my head down to look at her but couldn't see much of her face the way we were sitting.

"Yes. Thank you." Mia had her chin tipped down and her voice was soft and husky, but she didn't move away.

I started the fight up again and we watched for a bit, neither of us saying much. It didn't feel awkward, just quiet. Mia had been tensed up a bit, but eventually she relaxed against me. I was glad she wasn't asking questions about the fight because I was having a hell of a time concentrating on it. I was fighting to keep my hands still and not give in to the urge to run them over Mia's back and legs. I wanted to bury my face in her hair, but I settled for breathing in the light scent of her shampoo. She fit perfectly in my arms and it felt like she was made to be there. I was surprised a few minutes later when Mia's head rested fully on my shoulder, then she nuzzled her face into my neck. My dick had been half hard before that, but at the feel of Mia's face against my neck it instantly became fully rock hard. I heard Mia's soft, regular breathing and realized she was asleep. It was the sweetest kind of torture holding her against me, dick aching, unable to touch her or kiss her the way my body and mind were begging me to. I knew I should wake her up so she could get some rest in her own bed, but I couldn't make myself let her go. I switched off the TV, carefully turned a little sideways still holding on to Mia, lifted my legs up onto the couch, and rested my head on the wide, soft arm of the couch. Mia shifted a little then settled right back down. Mia was laying partly on top of me, and partly tucked between my body and the back of the couch. I knew that this might be a huge mistake, that Mia might freak out if she woke up wrapped up on my couch with me. As I drifted to sleep with Mia in my arms, I decided it was worth the risk.

Chapter 15

Mia

As I got ready for the sponsor event, my mind drifted again and again to that morning. I'd tried to stay busy all day to keep from thinking. But my mind kept returning to waking up slowly that morning and, as I did, coming to the realization that I was laying on top of Dante. My head was on his chest and his left arm was securely around my waist even in sleep. It was like he didn't want to let go, didn't want me to get away. I knew that was just my hopeful imagination, but I'd loved the feeling of being held so securely, like he wouldn't let anything come between us. He felt so good, his hard body stretched out underneath me, his hand resting on my hip, my head resting on his chest. When I tipped my chin up a bit, my mouth almost brushed his neck. I wanted to kiss him there, to feel his skin against my lips, to see if he tasted as good as he felt. I wanted to run my mouth over his jaw and feel his slight stubble. My left hand rested on his chest and I wanted to run it over him, to trace his firm body, slip my hand under his shirt and feel his warm skin.

The longer I lay there imagining all the things I'd like to do to Dante, the more I realized that I really needed to get up. I hadn't meant to fall asleep on Dante the night before, but a long week and a couple of drinks had caught up to me. Poor guy had just been trying to help me out so I wasn't freezing. I'd been so warm and comfortable

I'd just nodded off. I guess if Dante had wanted to get rid of me, he could have just woken me up and sent me back to my own apartment, so hopefully he hadn't minded too much. But falling asleep on him accidentally and continuing to lay here on top of him awake were two totally different things. The first could still fit into the "friend" category, the second most certainly could not. If Dante woke up and realized I was awake but still laying there tangled up with him I would be mortified. Moving slowly, I slipped out of Dante's hold and moved off of him to sit on the edge of the coffee table. I was stiff from being in the same position for a while and it took my muscles a minute to recover. As the stiffness eased, I watched Dante. It was still early, the light soft, but enough to see. Dante continued to sleep peacefully, for which I was eternally grateful. He had his right arm flung up over his head and just looking at the way his bicep stretched the sleeve of his shirt made me drool just a little. His face was relaxed in sleep and it hit me how beautiful he was. When he was awake his dark eyes and gorgeous smile always kept my attention, but without those favorite distractions I could sit in the quiet and absorb how truly handsome and compelling his features were. I was already reaching out a hand to trace his soft lips when I came to my senses and stopped myself. Sitting here staring at Dante while he slept wasn't much better than continuing to lay on the couch with him. I needed to get back to my own apartment before this turned into a really embarrassing situation. It wouldn't be easy to continue to ignore the growing attraction I felt for Dante now that I knew what it felt like to be in his arms, but I needed to do just that. The best thing I could do was be a great friend and help him pull off this pretend date tonight and secure some sponsors for the youth program. The last thing he needed was me giving into my crush on him when he had an important night ahead of him.

Leaving Dante sleeping on his couch I slipped out quietly and let myself back into my own apartment. As I crawled into bed to get a little more sleep, I realized I was still wearing Dante's sweatshirt. It was soft and smelled like him. I pulled it close around me, burrowed under the covers, and drifted off to sleep.

⌒

I was just finishing up getting ready for the sponsor event when I heard a knock on my door. It seemed like it had taken forever to get ready, but I'd been texting Meg periodically with progress updates while she texted me with encouragement. She was convinced that Dante wanted me and was going to lose his mind when he saw me tonight. I was convinced I had the best friend in the world. She was apparently delusional, but no one was a bigger cheerleader for me. Getting ready had also taken so long because I'd done a lot of primping I didn't normally do. I had full make-up on, I'd added some curls to enhance the natural curl of my hair, and in the shower I'd shaved…well, everything. It was silly, I knew. It wasn't like Dante was going to know whether I'd shaved or not. But I'd know and for some reason, that mattered tonight. I was also wearing a new dove gray lace demi push-up bra that actually gave me a little cleavage and a matching thong. Again, Dante would never know I had them on, but they made me feel a little sexy and confident. Meg had talked me into buying them earlier in the week along with the outfit I was wearing.

Dante had been spectacularly unhelpful when I'd asked him earlier in the week about what to wear to the event. His first response, *Whatever you want. You always look nice,* was lovely and sweet. It was also completely untrue, since I knew I often looked barely presentable in baggy sweatshirts and leggings or yoga pants. It also didn't get me any closer to knowing what to wear. I'd pressed for more specifics and his response had basically been not formal, not t-shirt and jeans, but somewhere in between. Again, sooo not helpful.

Meg and I had put our heads together and found an outfit that I felt comfortable enough in, but that Meg also assured me was smokin' hot. I thought that was pushing it a bit, but I did think I looked pretty good. I was wearing a soft shimmery gray sweater with a deep loose scoop neck paired with a slim black skirt that stopped several inches above my knees and black heels. The 3 ½ inch heels were higher than I typically wore, but I could get away with them given Dante's height. And even I had to admit, my long legs looked good in the skirt and heels. I wore a simple silver necklace and earrings with a bit of sparkle. Meg assured me that the outfit wasn't too dressy or too plain or too… anything. I hoped she was right because Dante was here and there was no turning back now.

Reaching my door, I stopped, took a deep breath, and opened it with a smile. I was determined that things would not be awkward just because I'd spent the night sleeping on Dante's couch with him. I would not make the mistake of thinking it meant anything.

As soon as I saw Dante, my brain screeched to a halt. He stood outside my door looking like sex personified. He had on a black button-down shirt that fit him perfectly, showcasing his wide shoulders, muscular arms and torso, and slim waist. It was untucked and he had the sleeves rolled up just a bit, showing off his spectacular forearms. I didn't know what it was about that that made me even hotter than just seeing his arms bared in a t-shirt, but wow, that look really worked for him. He had paired the shirt with dark jeans that hugged his hips and thighs. I was looking forward to seeing him from behind because I bet his butt looked fantastic.

As I had that thought I realized three things: One, I was standing there not saying a word; two, I was staring; and three, Dante was staring right back. His dark eyes roamed over my face and body, seemingly noting every detail. He wasn't smiling. His face looked hard, his jaw tight, and as he finally met my eyes his were intense.

"You look absolutely fucking amazing."

Dante's voice was rough and gravelly. His hands clenched, then he stepped back and took a deep breath, as if he was settling himself down. He seemed really on edge. Was he nervous about tonight? Time to be a good friend and get us both through this.

"Thank you, that's nice of you to say." I smiled at him, wanting to ease his tension. "You clean up pretty good yourself."

"Thanks," he returned, still not smiling but seeming a little calmer. "You ready to go?"

I pulled my coat off the coat rack by the door and Dante held it for me while I slipped it on and freed my long hair. I grabbed my phone and we were out the door.

When we reached Dante's truck, I realized that I had an issue. He held open the truck door for me, but the truck sat high and with the short tight skirt I had on, there was no way I could get in gracefully. I looked over my shoulder at Dante. He stood right behind me, and as I turned my head to look at him, I noticed how close our mouths were with my additional height from my heels. If I just leaned toward him a little bit…

"What's wrong?" Dante's voice was still rough. I could feel the heat from his body on my back and it made me want to lean back into him.

I somehow got control of myself and looked down at my skirt. "I have a bit of an issue. I can't get in the truck with this skirt on."

"Ah." I could feel Dante's exhale against my cheek. "Got it. Turn around."

I turned around to face him then squeaked in surprise as he put his hands on my hips and lifted me into the truck seat. His hands lingered for a second as if he were making sure I was set before he let me go. Once he stepped back, I swung my legs into the truck. Dante shut the door, then walked around to the driver's side and climbed in.

"Sorry I fell asleep on you last night." I'd decided not to say anything about it in case it was awkward but apparently my brain had other ideas.

Dante glanced over as he started his truck and drove out of our lot. There, finally, was a small smile. "Don't worry about it. I think we were just both beat from a long week."

"I have your sweatshirt. I'll return it once I've had a chance to do laundry." I really didn't want to either wash it or return it. It was soft and smelled like Dante. I wanted to keep it the way it was and cuddle up in bed with it.

"I'm not worried about it." Another smile. Good, maybe he was starting to relax. "You can keep it if you want. It looks better on you anyway."

I had no idea what to say to that, so I changed the subject to something I'd been wondering about.

"I was thinking...is there anybody else who's going to be there tonight that I should know? Other than your ex and her boyfriend, I mean? Other people I should know about?"

Dante nodded. "Dev and his girlfriend, Nicole, will be there. If you see a tall guy with a beard who's a little bigger than me with a girl with long wavy blond hair, that's them. Of course, I'm going to be glued to your side the whole night, right? So I'll introduce you when we see them."

I laughed as I remembered our deal. "That's right, no ditching me and no speeches. Anybody else?"

"Not necessarily. I'll know a lot of people and they'll know me, but there's no reason you would know them."

"Okay. So, how did we meet? What's our story?"

Dante glanced over at me. "Do we *need* a story?"

I turned toward him a bit in my seat. "Will there be any other women at this event that we might talk to?" At Dante's "Yeah, of course." I went on. "One of the first things a woman who knows you is going to ask when she meets me, the person you're supposedly dating, is how we met."

"Huh." Dante shook his head as if women mystified him. "Why don't we just stick as close to basic facts as possible? We met because we're neighbors, we started talking, then started dating a couple of weeks ago. That's at least partly true."

Too bad it was the dating part that was the lie. I swallowed that down and went on. "First date?"

"Uh…we haven't really gone out on a date yet because of our busy schedules? That makes me sound like a loser that I haven't actually taken you out, but I'll take the hit."

"I think your reputation will recover."

Dante shot me a grin that could melt the panties right off a girl. I was still recovering when I realized he was talking again.

"You know what I don't know much about? You. Your background, I mean. I know where you work, that you used to do massage – and still kick ass at it – that Meg is your best friend, and that you've lived here about two years. Oh, and that you were sadly ignorant about boxing until very recently. That's it. What else should I know?"

"Hmm…let's see. Well, you know I'm twenty-four and still don't know what I want to be when I grow up. And you know that I'm typically super shy. See?" I looked over at Dante. "You know more than you thought you did." Dante glanced back with a smile.

"True. Keep going."

"I grew up in a small town about two hours northwest of here. My parents still live there. I was really, really shy growing up. So much so I would barely talk to people. I met Meg in third grade. She moved to town right before school started. The first day of class, she walked in, sat down beside me, and decided to be my best friend. We were inseparable as kids. Fast forward a few years, Meg moved here for college, then stayed here for her job. I followed her here a couple years ago. I've been trying to overcome my shyness for a long time. I'd think I was doing fine but I was too isolated in my small town. I needed to be somewhere surrounded by people I hadn't known most of my life. So…here I am."

Dante glanced over when I stopped talking, then grinned when I didn't continue. "That's definitely the short version, but I guess it gets the job done for tonight. I want to hear the rest of the story sometime, though."

"Sure" I shrugged. My life story was pretty boring stuff, but Dante was being nice saying he wanted to hear it, so I played along.

"One last question. What's your go-to drink when you're out? I've seen you drink both wine and beer. Do you have a preference? That seems like something I should know."

"I usually go with chardonnay. It's pretty standard and it's typically at least decent."

"Chardonnay, got it."

Just as he said it, Dante pulled up in front of the hotel where the event was being held. It wasn't the hotel where I worked, which I'd been happy to hear when Dante told me the location. The last thing I needed was teasing from my co-workers while I was trying to stay calm and collected for Dante.

Dante pulled into the short line of cars waiting for valet parking, then smiled over at me. "You ready to have some fun?"

I looked back at him, eyebrows raised.

"Oh, is that what we're doing tonight?" I was half joking, but only half.

"What the hell, let's give it a try. These events are usually a pretty good time. We'll have to talk to few sponsors, shake some hands, that kind of thing, but other than that, let's just try to enjoy the night. What do you say?"

Dante looked over at me intently, like he thought he needed to convince me.

"Sure, why not? Let's try."

"That's my girl," Dante said as he pulled up the last few feet and put the car in park for the valet. I knew it was just an expression, but my heart jumped a little at his words anyway. I was really starting to wish those words were true. "Hang on a sec and I'll be around to help you down."

The valet opened my door for me, but I waited for Dante to come around the truck before turning in my seat. Dante stepped close and lifted me out of the truck, setting me on my feet gently. I looked up to thank him, our eyes met, and time stopped.

Dante's eyes...his lips...were so close. I noticed again as I had earlier that all I had to do was lean in, lift my chin a little, and my mouth would be on Dante's. His big, warm hands gripped my waist and my hands rested on his biceps. We were suspended in time, neither of us breathing. Dante's eyes burned into mine with a look I'd never seen before. Then a car door slammed and we were jarred out of our trance.

Dante stepped back, his hands falling from my waist and mine falling to my side. I turned to grab my phone out of the truck where I'd nearly forgotten it and when I turned back, my friend Dante was back in place. He'd taken a step back and there was no sign that our moment had even happened.

He gave me his familiar smile and held out his hand. "Ready?"

I answered truthfully, "As I'll ever be" and slipped my hand into his.

"Then here we go." He pulled my hand through his arm to rest on his forearm, then tucked his arm close to his body. My left side, shoulder to hip, was pressed close to him as we walked toward the hotel entrance. Dante was solid and warm next to me, slowing his steps a bit to accommodate my shorter stride and the heels I was wearing. My heart yearned to make this real, to be able to say that this gorgeous, funny, hard-working, thoughtful guy was mine. I got to pretend for a little bit tonight and I resolved to make the most of it. Hopefully, I'd left shy Mia at home and would give Dante the fun night he wanted.

Chapter 16

Dante

This night was fucking torture. I was so hyper aware of Mia's every move, every sound, I felt like I was constantly being brushed by a live wire. When she'd opened the door of her apartment, I swear I almost passed out as all the blood in my body rushed to my dick. It was a good thing my untucked shirt helped to cover my crotch. It was all I could do to even carry on a conversation. I knew the way I'd tensed up had puzzled Mia. I could see it in her eyes. I'd managed to get it under control a little on the drive with Mia's calm presence and sweet voice soothing my tension as always. But when we'd arrived and I'd lifted her out of the truck…the need to press my body into hers, thread my hand into her hair, and kiss the holy hell out of her had been almost overwhelming. She'd looked up at me, brown eyes a little stunned like she felt the same insane pull I did. Her lips had parted just a bit and I'd almost leaned in and taken her mouth right there in front of the valets and God knows who else. If the slam of a car door hadn't jolted me back to reality, I'd have kissed Mia senseless and wouldn't have wanted to stop there.

As it was, I was barely hanging on by a thread. I'd spent the last hour with Mia by my side, standing close enough for me to keep my hand on her hip or back most of the time. It was all part of our act, but nothing had ever felt more natural than touching Mia. I'd noticed the looks of interest Mia was getting from some of the other men and I was doing my best to shut that shit down by staying close to her and giving them a look that clearly told them they'd only get to Mia through me. I'd have done something more blatant, but I didn't want to embarrass Mia.

While I suffered, Mia was doing fantastic. I could see her fighting her natural shyness at moments, but I doubted anyone else picked up on it. She smiled her sweet smile and made a comment here or there in her quiet way and everyone seemed to love her. We'd talked to a couple of sponsors already and gotten a good vibe from them about the youth program. No solid commitments yet, but I was sure we'd have one soon. We'd already been asked twice how we met – both times by women – which had earned me an "I told you so" nudge in my side from Mia each time. We'd been at the event for more than an hour and hadn't run into Dev and Nicole yet. Dev had texted that they'd arrived a bit ago, so Mia and I decided to take a break from schmoozing to look for them. The good news was that there had been no sign of Haven and Justin yet, which was more than fine with me. If we could somehow get through the night without running into them at all, it would be perfect.

We finally found Dev and Nicole on the upper level of the huge room near one of the bars in a quieter area with some high-top tables and stools. It was a little less crowded and we managed to grab a table and a couple of stools for the girls. Dev and I headed to bar for drinks. I'd told Mia I wouldn't leave her, but she needed a minute to get off her feet and she said she'd be fine with Nicole.

As Dev and I waited at the bar, we traded notes on which sponsors we'd talked to and what the response had been. We were both confident we'd have at least one to two solid sponsorship deals for the expansion of the youth program in the works within the next few weeks. There were a few sponsors at the event that neither of us had talked with yet and definitely wanted to, but we both felt really good about the conversations we'd already had.

"How's the "date" going?" Dev asked after we'd made it up to the bar and given our order. He didn't make the air quotes motion with his hands, but you could hear it in his voice.

"Mia's doing great and everybody loves her."

Dev eyed me as the bartender handed over our beers and went back for the girls' drinks.

"Yeah? I hear a 'but'…"

"But she's driving me crazy. I can barely keep my hands off her. We were talking to the Webers and all I could think about was what Mia would do if I reached out and ran my hand over her ass. Thank God Mr. Weber and Mia were talking about the benefits of hot stone massage or something like that and were oblivious, but from the look in Mrs. Weber's eye she caught on to the fact that my mind was on Mia's ass, not the conversation."

"Eh, Mrs. Weber's cool." The Webers were fixtures in the local boxing community. They knew everyone and pretty much everything that was going on. They were an insanely rich couple, but you would never know it from their low-key manner. "If she thinks you're smitten with Mia she'll eat that shit up."

The bartender came back with Mia's wine and Nic's sparkling water. As we grabbed the drinks and turned to head back to the table, Dev eyed me again.

"The question is *are* you smitten?"

"I don't know, man, I'm something. Smitten? Maybe, whatever the hell that is. Fucking obsessed is more like it. If I can just get through tonight, I'm going to lay it all out for Mia, tell her I want her. This friends and neighbors shit isn't enough anymore."

As we made our way back to the table with drinks, I could see Nicole was saying something to Mia, a wistful look on her face. I knew she and Dev were having problems and I wondered if that's what the girls were talking about. Nicole had only known Mia for about 15 minutes so it would be a little odd to have such a personal conversation but Nic was a bit different in everything she did. As Nicole looked up and saw us her sad expression dropped away and she quickly smiled as if everything was fine. She said something to Mia and Mia turned in her chair a bit to watch us approach.

I handed Mia her chardonnay and she took it with a smile that made me feel like we'd just shared an inside joke. I stood next to her and rested a hand on the seatback of her stool, fighting the urge to play with her hair. Nic excused herself to run to the ladies' room and Dev and I talked a bit about two of the fighters from the gym who had competitions coming up. We were in the middle of explaining to Mia how the format of the competitions worked when Nicole returned, looking worried.

"Sorry to be the bearer of bad news, but Justin and Haven are here. I saw them come in downstairs."

At Nicole's words Mia turned to look at me. When her eyes met mine, I saw concern. I knew it was concern for me. She was worried how Haven and Justin's appearance was going to hit me, if it would set me on edge just knowing that they were in the building. I was surprised to realize that it didn't impact me as much as I thought it would. I was never happy to be in the same space as them and I still hoped we could avoid them, but if we couldn't we'd deal with it and move on. I felt confident that I'd be able to keep it under control, no matter what Haven or Justin tried to start.

I gave in to my earlier urge to touch Mia's hair, giving the back a light tug as I held her eyes and answered her unspoken question.

"It's okay. I'm not worried about it. We'll do fine."

Her eyes lingered on my face for a few seconds like she was still checking on me, then she nodded and turned away to take a sip of her wine.

We changed the topic to other things and Nicole soon had us laughing as she told us about some crazy documentary she'd seen about a man who collected vampire memorabilia from all over the world and stored it all in a house he'd had built next door to his own. Dev was a pretty serious guy most of the time, but she even got a smile out of him. It was the perfect thing to loosen all of us up and get our minds off the stress of sponsors and exes for a few minutes. I knew Nicole had done it on purpose. She was great at sensing the mood of a group and knowing just what to do to make it better if needed.

We were all still laughing as we finished our drinks and decided we should head back down to the main event area to make the rounds again. We decided to split up so we could talk with more people and meet up again in about an hour to start the real fun of the evening. These events could get pretty wild in the later hours what with all of the free alcohol that was flowing, so it was best to take care of business now while it was still relatively under control.

We stopped at the top of the wide staircase that curved down to the main area below. Mia wanted to hit the ladies' room on the upper floor so after a quick "see you later" to Nicole and Dev, she headed off. Before Nic and Dev headed down the stairs, Dev turned to me, his expression grim again.

"Watch your back. You know they'll be looking for you."

I knew he meant Haven and Justin and I knew he was right. As much as I hoped they would grow up and just leave the bullshit alone, I knew they wouldn't.

"I know. I'm ready," I assured him.

At this point I knew I'd keep things locked down as much or more for Mia's sake as for mine. If I lost my shit, Mia would not only feel like she'd failed me, she'd also be embarrassed as hell. She'd battled back her shyness for me tonight and was doing amazing. There was no way I was going to let anything I did ruin that.

I stood near the top of the stairs waiting for Mia and watching the crowd below. It was even more packed than when we'd escaped upstairs. I was going to have to keep Mia close to me to avoid losing her in the crush. I couldn't help the smile that thought brought to my face.

A second later my smile disappeared as my eyes landed on Haven in the crowd below. She was the center of attention of a group near the middle of the room, Justin standing next to her looking bored. She was dressed in a skintight sparkly dress cut low in the front and just barely long enough to cover her ass. She had a martini in her hand, her drink of choice, and I could tell she was already well on her way to being trashed. As I watched her laugh, I swore I could almost hear it from where I stood. I wondered if those around her could see how calculating her eyes were. Even from here I could see her making assessments of those around her, deciding who was worth her time and who wasn't. I counted myself lucky that I had nothing to do with her anymore. A woman like Mia was fucking priceless compared to the shallow, vain train wreck that was Haven Day.

"Oh my God, is that Haven?" Mia's voice startled me. I hadn't realized she'd joined me.

My eyes still on Haven, I nodded. "Yeah, in all her glory."

I turned to look at Mia. She was staring down at Haven, looking shocked and mesmerized like she couldn't look away. Before I could get another word out, Mia turned to look at me. The disbelief and faint hurt in her eyes made my words stick in my throat.

"You didn't tell me she's stunning, Dante." That was definitely hurt and a little bit of panic I heard in her voice. "I figured she was probably beautiful, but you didn't tell me she's perfect. How am I supposed to face that? Who in the hell is going to believe that you went from her..." Mia flung her hand in Haven's direction, then brought it back to point at herself,"...to me? Seriously, Dante, you couldn't have warned me?"

Mia's voice was rising a bit and she was definitely starting to panic. I pulled her away from the top of the stairs and steered us toward a small alcove that was a little out of the way. It wasn't exactly private, but it would have to do. When we reached the alcove, I pulled Mia in front of me, facing me with her back to the wall, so that I blocked her from the view of anyone walking by. All they would see was my back, not the look of distress on Mia's face. She looked down at the floor, shoulders slumped and hands clenched, like she didn't know whether to fight or admit defeat.

"Mia, look at me." I didn't want her to think I was upset with her so I said it as gently as I could. When I got no response, I reached out and tilted her face up to mine. I needed to see her eyes to know how to fix this. And I desperately needed to fix it. I couldn't stand that she thought she was less than Haven in any way. That couldn't be further from the truth.

When Mia's eyes met mine, I saw dejection and resignation. Though I held her face in my hand so she couldn't dip her head again, Mia's eyes slid away from mine.

"Mia, please, I need you to look at me." I could hear the pleading note in my voice, but I didn't care. "I need to know that you're hearing me. Please."

Mia's eyes slid back up to mine. She seemed reluctant, but she held my gaze.

"I'm sorry." I said softly, hoping she would hear the sincerity behind my words. "I'm sorry I didn't prepare you well enough for the reality of Haven. I just honestly didn't think of it. I know objectively she's beautiful..." I regretted my choice of words at Mia's quick intake of breath and the shadows gathering in her eyes. I rushed on. "But that's not what I see. She's a pretty shell with nothing inside. However attractive she may seem on the outside, there's nothing attractive about her on the inside."

Mia shifted. Afraid that she was going to try to slip away from me, I put my hand on her other cheek, framing her face between my hands. I needed to make her understand.

"Mia, she's nothing compared to you. Nothing. It's like you're not even on the same planet."

"Dante." Mia shook her head the tiniest bit, disbelief in her eyes and in her voice.

"You're the one who's stunning, Mia. I know you don't know that, much less believe it. But you are. And the more someone gets to know you, the more beautiful you are, inside and out."

"That's sweet of you to say, Dante. It really is." I slid my hands down to Mia's shoulders and she finally touched me, resting her hands on my arms. "But Haven looks like a model. She's not just pretty, she's perfect. She exudes confidence even from across the room. She's everything I'm not."

"You're right that she's a lot of things you're not and none of them are good. You might see confidence. In reality, she's vain, shallow and self-absorbed. All that matters to her is her. Other people are a means to an end. It took me too long to see it, but it's true. It wouldn't even occur to her to offer to help a neighbor. If you asked, she'd laugh. She would never, never help someone like you've stepped up to help me."

Mia was starting to look a little less dejected, like maybe she was beginning to hear me.

"I don't know." Mia sighed. "I still don't think people will really believe you went from her to me. Not once they see us side-by-side." Mia dropped her hands from my arms and stepped back a little. She didn't go far, bumping into the wall at her back.

I couldn't make myself let her go yet. I needed to touch her, needed the connection. Sometime in the last minute I'd decided to take the leap. Screw my plan to take it slow with Mia after tonight and see where things went. I was going to lay my cards on the table right here and now. I stepped a little closer and put my hands on Mia's hips. She looked up at me in question, no doubt wondering what the hell I was doing. There was no one nearby, so no need to pretend. What she didn't know was that the time for pretending was over.

"The only reason they wouldn't believe we're together is because you're completely out of my league." She didn't believe me. I could see it. I needed to take the big jump.

"I tricked you into coming with me tonight, Mia," I confessed. "I hope you can forgive me for that." I forced myself to meet Mia's eyes, while she looked back at me, her frown making a little crease between her eyebrows. I wanted to lean forward and kiss it away, but I kept on talking. "I wanted you to be here to help me stay in control, that much is true. But mostly I just wanted you to be here. I had no idea how you saw me, how you see me, if you really just want me as a friend or what, but I couldn't take the chance you'd turn me down, so I asked you to pretend you're with me."

I stopped to take a breath. The words had been rushing out. Mia was looking at me, but I couldn't read her expression at all. My heart pounding, I went on.

"That's where I lied to you, Mia." I held her eyes with mine and gripped her hips a little tighter. She wasn't pulling away, but she wasn't touching me either. "None of this has been pretend for me. I haven't been acting when I touch you or stand close to you or hold your hand. I'm doing all of those things because I want to. Since I'm being honest, I want to do a lot more. I have for weeks. I'm sorry I did things the way I did and didn't just ask you to come with me for real. I was afraid you would say no and I'd miss my chance before I'd even had it."

I forced myself to stop. I watched Mia and as the silence stretched between us, I could feel my chest constrict. Had I fucked up complete-ly? Would Mia pull away, walk out on me, and never look back? What was going on in her head?

Finally, I couldn't stand it anymore.

"Mia, say something. Tell me you understand. Tell me to go fuck myself. Anything." I sounded desperate, but fuck it, I was.

"I…" Mia closed her eyes and raised her hand to rub her forehead. "It's a lot to process."

"I know. I'm sorry. Are you mad at me?"

"No." Mia opened her eyes and lowered her hand, resting it on my arm like she had earlier. I started to breathe again. She glanced up at me, then dropped her gaze to my chest. I was sure she could see my heart still pounding.

"I'm not mad. I'm just…overwhelmed."

"Okay." I blew out a breath in relief. We weren't all right yet, but maybe we could get there. "I know I threw a lot at you. I'd never want to lose you as a friend, but I want a lot more. If the thought of that doesn't make you want to run screaming, we can figure out together what it means."

Mia huffed out a tiny laugh. Okay, this was good.

"Does that part at least make sense?"

"It does. I think." Mia finally, finally met my eyes. She took a deep breath. With her cheeks turning a little pink, she said the words I needed more than anything to hear. "I like you, too, Dante. If you lied, I did, too. I haven't been pretending tonight either."

She couldn't have any idea how those words rocked me. A wave of relief and adrenaline rushed through me. She didn't hate me, she wasn't running away from me, and craziest of all, she seemed to want more with me, too.

The urge to pull her into me and cover her mouth with mine was so strong my hands shook. I wanted to consume her, devour her, become her entire focus the way that she'd become mine. But she'd only said she liked me, that she wanted to be more than a friend, not that she wanted to be mauled in a public place. As much as I wanted to take Mia home, rush her into my bed, and slip inside her for hours, I knew we couldn't. That was way too much, way too fast. And we still had the rest of this night to get through.

I settled for pulling Mia close and wrapping my arms around her. I kept my hold light, not wanting to overwhelm her any more. It felt so fucking good. When I felt Mia's arms come around me, I swear I heard a 'click' like the last piece of a puzzle had been snapped into place. I kissed Mia softly on the side of her head, inhaling the light scent of her hair, then made myself loosen my hold a little and step back so I could see her face again.

"As much as I'd like to leave right now, take you home, and figure this out with you tonight, I can't. We need to get through the rest of this event. Let's start over, okay? For the rest of the night, we're on a real date. We're together for real, no pretending needed. Are you okay with that?"

Mia nodded up at me, still in my hold with her arms loosely around my waist. "Yes, I'd like that. I know we can't just bail. Let's try to have fun like we said before, okay?"

"It's a plan. Let the fun begin." Mia smiled and I couldn't resist pulling her close for another quick kiss on her temple. I slid my hand down to hers and linked our fingers as we walked towards the stairs. It was almost a shock to see the party still in full swing. We had been in our own little world in the alcove, just the two of us as everything else had faded away. I paused for a second at the top of the stairs, smiling down at Mia and asking her the same question I had when we'd arrived earlier. We were officially starting this date over.

"Ready?"

Mia caught on, realizing the significance of the question. She nodded firmly and tightened her hand on mine. "As I'll ever be."

"That's my girl," I said as I had earlier. And this time it felt like the truth.

Chapter 17

Mia

I walked down the stairs next to Dante, holding his hand and feeling like I was in a dream. My head was still swirling from everything he'd said. Dante wanted to be more than just friends? He had for weeks? Was I in a parallel universe? In my world, guys like Dante didn't go for the shy, awkward girls like me. I still didn't buy all of that stuff about me being stunning and gorgeous. Please, I looked in the mirror every morning. I knew what the reality was. I wasn't unattractive and on a good day I may even get close to pretty. But stunning? That wasn't me. It really was sweet of Dante to claim otherwise. He seemed sincere and that's what counted.

I thought back to what Nicole had said to me earlier as we waited on Dante and Dev to get back from the bar. She hadn't been specific, but she'd said enough that it was clear she and Dev were having some issues. She talked about finding "the one" then shocked me by saying, "Like you and Dante have. You're seamless together, like two halves of a whole." When I'd told her it wasn't like that, she was adamant. "Dante looks at you like you're his whole world. You may not see it but it's there. I wish..." She'd looked up and had apparently seen the guys on their way back to us. She stopped talking, her sadness dropped away, and she smiled like she was having a great time. I felt bad for her, and for Dev. Whatever was going on, neither one seemed happy. As

I thought back to her words, I had to give her credit. Nicole seemed really perceptive and she'd seen something in Dante's reactions to me that I had missed. As for the rest of it – the parts about finding "the one" and being Dante's whole world – I had to file that away to think about later. It was too much to process right now.

We were almost down the stairs when I felt Dante stiffen.

"We've been spotted. Haven saw us coming down the stairs. I'm sure we'll see her and Justin soon." I was glad that Dante didn't seem stressed about it, just…ready.

"Oh, perfect." I said with fake enthusiasm. "I'm so hoping to get a chance to meet them tonight."

Dante chuckled and I smiled in response. We made our way into the crowd, stopping to talk with a couple of other fighters that Dante knew. We moved on after a few minutes and a large man standing a short distance away waved at Dante, gesturing for us to come over to him. It seemed a little arrogant to me – he could have just walked over to where we stood – but Dante raised his hand in response and we headed in the man's direction. As we got closer, a couple we'd spoken to earlier, the Webers, joined the man, as well.

We reached the group and Dante exchanged a handshake with the man who had called us over. His other hand still in mine, Dante turned to introduce me. "Mia, this is Jock Landen, owner of Landen Sports and one of the gym's longest-running sponsors."

Holy cow, even people who had no interest in sports knew Landen Sports. They had several locations across the area. The huge stores sold every type of sportswear and equipment possible and their colorful purple and green signs were everywhere. The man had to have more money than some small countries. What could I possibly have to say to someone like him? Not to mention that he was obviously an important sponsor. Breathe, I told myself. Just as I thought that, I heard Dante say, "Jock, this is my girlfriend, Mia." The added shock of hearing Dante introduce me as his girlfriend didn't help my composure at all. I knew I needed to say something, but my words were stuck. Oh God, this was what I'd been afraid of. I was going to embarrass Dante. Just then, Mrs. Weber caught my eye. She winked at me and gave me an almost imperceptible nod. It was like she saying, "Come on, girl. You can do it." It was enough to snap me out of my spiral. All I had to do was say hello. One step at a time.

I looked up, way up, at Mr. Landen and smiled. Hopefully, it looked more natural than it felt. "Hello, Mr. Landen. It's a pleasure to meet you." There, that sounded normal. Dante squeezed my hand and I felt like I'd won a prize.

"Oh, now, no need to be formal. You can call me Jock." Jock's eyes were kind and I could see fondness in them as he looked at Dante. "I've known Dante and Dev for most of their lives, and Dev's uncle for a long time before that."

"That's right," Mr. Weber chimed in. "Jock's been around boxing even longer than we have. He's the one who got Lettie and me interested years ago." He looked at his wife, amusement on his face. "Lettie wasn't a fan at first, but she came around."

Mrs. Weber rolled her eyes and laughed as she looked over at me. "That was many, many years ago but he just loves to tell people that. I'll never live it down."

The Webers' good natured teasing and Jock's casual, friendly manner, despite my first impression of him, immediately relaxed me. I mentioned that I'd known almost nothing about boxing until recently, and Dante jumped into to say what a quick and curious learner I'd been once I'd given it a try. If you left out the part where I'd fallen asleep on him, I supposed that was true. We spent several minutes chatting, then Mr. Weber's gaze shifted to a point beyond Dante's shoulder. His eyes sharpened and he looked directly at Dante.

"Incoming. Behind you."

Just then, a loud female voice said "Dante!" with even more fake enthusiasm than I'd used when I'd joked about how eager I was to meet Haven tonight. It looked like I was about to get my chance.

Dante shifted to the side, tucking me behind him as if he was shielding me. I'd been standing between Jock and Dante; now I stood between Mr. Weber and Dante. Jock had slid over to Dante's other side, putting himself between Dante and Haven. A man I assumed was Justin stood between Haven and Mrs. Weber, completing our circle. The swap of places had been so smooth it almost seemed choreographed, although of course it wasn't. The end result was that Dante had placed me as far as he could get me from Haven, and Jock had created a buffer from Haven on the other side of Dante.

Dante didn't respond to Haven's greeting. I looked up at him. His jaw was a tiny bit tight, but his expression was indifferent. He didn't look like he cared one way or the other that his ex and the man she'd cheated with had joined us. If he was feeling stressed at their presence, he was doing a good job hiding it.

"Haven, Justin," Jock stepped into the void left by Dante's silence. "You know Dante and the Webers, of course." Mr. And Mrs. Weber nodded politely at Haven and Justin; Dante didn't respond in any way that I could tell. "And this is Dante's girlfriend, Mia."

Haven's expression changed to one of exaggerated surprise. She stared at me, a sharp smile on her face. "Girlfriend? Really?" Her disbelief was clear in her voice. "Well, that's just sweet. Justin, isn't that sweet?" Justin frowned down at the drink in his hand and said nothing. "How long have you two been together?" Her tone made what could have been a friendly question a challenge, instead.

I felt Dante shift next to me. "Leave it alone, Haven. You don't care how long we've been together."

"Oh, but I do. I know you've been bitter since I left you. It's good to see you're moving on."

From what Dante had told me, he'd been the one to do the leaving. He just shook his head and didn't respond. Taking a quick breath, I jumped in. This was what I was here for, right?

"We're neighbors, so we've known each other for a while, but we just started dating recently."

Haven returned her sharp gaze to me, looking at me like I was a bug that she was thinking about squashing.

Mrs. Weber spoke up, helping this awkward as hell conversation along. I liked her more by the minute.

"Dante was just telling us how he's been teaching Mia all about boxing." She turned to smile at me. "You hadn't told us yet what you think of it, Mia."

"Oh, there's so much I still don't know. I think the biggest thing I learned is that it's much more complex than it appears on the surface. It's fascinating to watch with someone like Dante who can tell you what to look for." I looked up at Dante and his eyes burned into mine. I felt him rest his hand on my back and was glad for the physical connection to him. Trying to lighten the mood a little, I confessed with a smile, "Of course, I was a weenie when it came to watching Dante's fights, and I don't know how I'd do at a live fight yet, but I think the sport could grow on me like it did on you, Mrs. Weber."

"Well, you won't have to worry about watching Dante fight live, isn't that right, Dante?" I almost groaned. I'd left that topic wide open for Haven. I hadn't even thought about the fact that she and Justin had been trying to goad Dante into fighting again. Dammit. Dante's hand dropped from my back and I looked down to see his fist clenched at his side. I put my hand on his lower back and rubbed up and down slowly, hoping with my touch to convey how sorry I was for bringing up the worst possible subject.

Haven pinned me with her sharp gaze again. She waved her martini in Dante's direction, coming dangerously close to spilling it all over Jock. You could tell that it was far from her first martini of the night. "Did your *boyfriend* tell you how he conveniently decided to retire just as he would have had to fight Justin to defend his title?" The thick sarcasm when she said the word "boyfriend" made me want to punch her, but I forced myself to maintain my calm expression and stay relaxed. Dante stiffened, so I kept moving my hand in small strokes on his lower back. Dante spoke, startling me after his silence.

"That's not what happened, and you know it." Dante's voice was a little strained, but he mostly sounded impatient. "You can tell whatever stories you want as often as you want, but that doesn't make them true."

"And you can deny it all you want but everyone knows you never would have won that title if you'd had to face Justin. You know it yourself or you would never have run away like a coward and done your best to ruin his chances of getting another shot." Haven's tone was getting heated now and her voice was rising. Heads were starting to turn our way. Haven threw back the rest of her martini, swaying a tiny bit.

"Now, listen..." Mr. Weber had just started to speak when Justin interrupted.

"Let it go, Haven. It doesn't matter anymore. It's old news."

Haven stared at Justin like she couldn't believe what she was hearing. I was with her on that one. I couldn't believe Justin was trying to get Haven to drop it. I looked up at Dante to see his reaction. His eyes, slightly narrowed, were focused on Justin.

"It does matter!" Haven was almost shrieking at this point. Thankfully, she'd finished her martini. With the way she was waving her hands around, we all would have been wearing it. "He cheated you out of your chance!"

Justin turned toward Haven, reaching out to grab her arm. "Stop. Just stop. I'm tired of hearing it and everyone else is, too. We're leaving, let's go."

Haven pulled her arm away from Justin and stomped her foot. I couldn't believe it. I'd never seen an adult stomp their foot like a child. Haven's pouty face went right along with the tantrum she was throwing. "Justin..." she whined.

"Young lady," Jock cut her off. "You'd do well to listen to Justin. It's time to move on, both from tonight's party and this delusion you have about Dante somehow cheating Justin. Out of respect for your father's memory we've all given you a pass for years, but you've worn out your welcome. Now listen to Justin and go on home before you embarrass yourself any more than you already have."

Haven looked at Jock in disbelief, then whirled to face Justin. "I can't believe you're letting him talk to me like that! Why are you just standing there?"

Without a word to any of us, Justin turned and walked away.

Haven called after him, "Justin. Justin!" When he didn't pause or turn around, she stomped her foot again, then turned her head to glare at all of us. "You're not worth my time anyway. Just has-beens and never-weres." She tossed her hair and started after Justin, still calling his name.

We all stood silent for a few seconds, watching Haven walk away. Without thinking I turned to Dante and asked, "You were with her for *how* long?" Dante leaned his head back and groaned. "Don't remind me. Way, way too long," he said, shaking his head. The pained expression on his face made all of us laugh, releasing the tension created by Haven's scene.

"Don't feel too bad." Mr. Weber looked from Dante to me and back. "We were all young and dumb once. What matters is you got it right this time." His pointed look at me made me blush. Dante ran his hand up my back and cradled the back of my neck, drawing my gaze to him. "I sure did." The look he gave me was soft and sweet. Without thinking I swayed closer to him and he slipped his arm around my shoulders.

"Well, ladies and gentlemen, I think that's enough fun for me." Jock's voice jolted me back to reality. For a few seconds I'd forgotten that Dante and I were in the middle of a crowded room. "I have one or two more people I need to track down, then I'm headed out." He shook Dante and Mr. Weber's hands, kissed me and Mrs. Weber on the cheek, and made his way into the crowd. After a few more minutes, the Webers said their good-byes, as well. As she gave me a hug Mrs. Weber said quietly in my ear, "He's crazy about you. He can barely take his eyes off you. Don't doubt yourself." Her words both reassured me and startled me. I hadn't meant to let my doubts show on my face. I just mouthed "thank you" and waved as she and Mr. Weber walked away.

I turned to Dante and just looked at him. He was so beautiful, so tall and strong. And he said he wanted to be with me. It felt like things had changed so much so quickly. It seemed impossible that it was just this morning that I'd woken up on Dante's couch with him.

Dante reached out and snagged one of my hands. He dipped his head a little to look into my eyes. "You okay?"

"I am," I reassured him. "You?"

"Perfect." His smile lit up his whole face and took my breath away. "The hard part is over. You ready to find Dev and Nicole and have some fun?"

"Yes, absolutely."

Dante texted Dev to see where he and Nicole were, and we headed to the nearest bar for a drink. I switched to sparkling water with lime, already buzzing enough from the events of the night without any more wine. Dev didn't text back right away, so we just kept our eye out for him and Nicole as we chatted with other people Dante knew. I caught Dante glancing my way often and he touched me constantly, not in an obnoxious or overbearing way, just like he wanted the physical contact with me. My thoughts went back to Mrs. Weber's words. Was Dante crazy about me? This whole night had been kind of crazy so maybe I should believe it was true.

Dev finally texted back, but Dante frowned down at the phone as he read the message. The way Nicole had been talking earlier I hoped she and Dev hadn't had a fight.

"Is everything okay?"

Dante looked up from his phone. "Yeah, probably. Dev's message is just a little weird. It says, *"We're near the bottom of the stairs with someone who's been looking for you."*

"Maybe it's a sponsor," I suggested.

"Maybe." Dante didn't look or sound convinced. "But why didn't he just say that?" He shrugged. "I guess we'll find out."

I held on to Dante's hand and pressed close to him as he made a path for us through the crowd. Though you could tell some people had left, the place was still packed. Before long we could see Dev's tall form near the stairs. Nicole stood nearby talking with another couple. Standing with Dev was a man who was several inches shorter and much heavier than Dev. He looked like someone who had been a big, athletic guy years ago in high school or college. Dev said something to him and he turned to watch us approach. I wanted to ask Dante if he recognized the man, but I didn't have time before we reached him and Dev.

"Mr. March, this is Dante Ortiz." Dante and Mr. March shook hands briefly, as Dev looked over at me. "And this is Mia Kelly."

"My girlfriend," Dante added. Dev's eyebrows shot up at that, but he didn't say anything as he continued the introductions.

"Dante, this is Silas March. You two apparently have a mutual friend. He's been informed that you're considering fighting again and wants to talk with you about it."

To my relief, Dante remained relaxed, still holding my hand, not tensing up at all. He shook his head.

"No, there's no truth to that at all. I don't know who told you that, Mr. March, but there's no chance of it happening."

"Silas. No chance at all? Not even if I could make you a very rich man, win or lose?" Silas' eyes narrowed on Dante's face as if he were trying to assess Dante's reaction.

Dante didn't hesitate. "I have plenty of money in the bank from my fighting days. I'm involved with the gym because I still love the sport of boxing and I love the work. But I don't need the money and I have no desire to fight again."

Silas glanced over at Dev. Dev smirked. "Told you so."

Silas nodded, a rueful look on his face. "That you did. I'm disappointed with your answer, Dante, but I can't say I'm surprised. The person who gave me the information assured me that he had an in with you, but he's been extremely difficult to pin down. I'd begun to suspect he was full of shit – pardon the language, miss – but I needed to be certain. I decided the best way to do that was to come tonight to talk with you myself."

Understanding dawned on Dante's face. "It's Pete Carson who's been telling you I'm thinking about fighting again, isn't it?"

"Yes, it is."

"I know Pete, but he doesn't have any kind of inside track on my life. Far from it. He's been bugging me for the last few months about fighting again. I've told him no about a dozen times."

"I see. I'm sorry he's been so persistent. That's likely my fault since I offered him a sizable finder's fee, if you will, if he secured your agreement to fight and made the introduction."

Dante nodded, then shifted as if something had occurred to him. "Do you drive a silver car with tinted windows?" I looked at him in surprise. That was the car Mrs. Curr had given me grief about. Why did he think that was connected to this?

Silas looked at Dante for a minute. "I don't, but one of my associates does. Why do you ask?"

"Because someone has been hanging out in a car like that in the parking lot of our apartment building. Just sitting with the car running like they're watching the place."

Silas smiled, but there was no humor in it. "Ah. Again, my apologies. It seems that one of my associates may have been overzealous in attempting to verify Pete's information. I'll make sure you're not bothered again." He pinned Dante with an intense gaze. He was being extremely polite, but he gave me the chills just the same. "You're certain I can't persuade you to consider my offer?"

Dante shook his head, not hesitating at all. "No. I'm flattered but I have no interest."

Silas inclined his head, accepting Dante's answer. "In that case, if you'll excuse me, I'll leave you to your evening."

With a final polite nod at the three of us, Silas turned and walked away. We stood watching him for a second.

"Well, at least we can tell Mrs. Curr she won't be bothered by that silver car anymore."

Dante laughed and Dev just looked confused. Before I could explain, Nicole walked over and joined us.

"Did you tell him no, Dante?"

"Of course. Those days are over."

"I didn't know Pete was still bugging you about fighting." Dev said. "I would have told him to stay the hell away from the gym all those times he was hanging around."

"Nah, it's no big deal. He's a pain in the ass but he's harmless." Dante wrapped his arm around my shoulders. It made me want to cuddle close to him and rest my head on his shoulder, but I resisted the urge.

"And speaking of harmless, we ran into Haven and Justin."

At Dante's words, Dev tensed up visibly. "Yeah? What's with the 'harmless' part?"

Dante and I looked at each other, then Dante looked back over at Dev. "Haven started stirring shit and Justin shut her down."

Dev surprise was obvious. "No shit? Maybe he's finally done with her crazy."

"He straight up walked away from her. We were standing with Jock and the Webers and between Justin walking off and Jock telling her to cut the crap, she ended up looking like an ass and storming off after Justin. We barely had to say a word." Dante smiled over at me. "Of course, Mia was ready to go a round or two with her, but it ended up she didn't need to."

I could feel my face heat as I blushed. "I wasn't ready to 'go a round'. I just didn't like the way she was talking to you." I sounded grumpy, even to myself.

Dev and Nicole grinned at me as Dante gave my shoulders a light squeeze.

"I'm sorry I missed that." Dev said as he held his fist out to me. Feeling like an idiot, I reached out and bumped it with my own. "Thanks for having Dante's back. Glad you all didn't have to throw down. And I'm glad she did it in front of Jock and the Webers. She was looking to embarrass you in front of some of the most important people here and instead she embarrassed herself."

"Karma." Nicole said quietly.

I smiled. "Of the best kind."

Dante laughed. "Definitely, the very best bite-you-in-the-ass kind. So...are you guys ready to relax?"

Nicole leaned on Dev and shook her head. "I feel like such a party pooper saying this, but I think I'm done. It's later than I realized and I have a yoga class to teach at 6am." She looked up at Dev. "Is it okay with you if we go?"

"Of course." Dev kissed her on the top of the head and took her hand. "You kids are on your own. Mia, it was a pleasure. I hope we'll be seeing a lot more of you."

Dante grunted at the very unsubtle statement from Dev, but I just smiled and leaned into Dante.

"You will be, I promise."

After a quick hug from Nicole, she and Dev headed out, leaving Dante and I standing alone. Dante turned toward me, sliding his hand down to my hip.

"You still hanging in there?"

Dante knew my feet had been hurting earlier. My heels were cute and I loved them, but they definitely weren't made for hours of standing. "I'd honestly love to get off my feet. If we could find a spot to sit for a bit, I'd be fine to hang out."

"Would you be disappointed if we head on home? Nic's right - it's later than I realized and we had a lot going on tonight. Getting out of the noise and the crowd actually sounds good."

I didn't realize how beat I was until Dante suggested heading home. I could have made it for a little longer, but I was glad I wouldn't have to.

"Oh well, you know what a party girl I am so I would usually close the place down, but for you I'll go home early just this once."

Dante laughed at my response and pulled me close for a second, then stepped back and held out his hand. "Alright, party girl. Let's get your coat."

We headed to the coat check and waited for them to find my coat among all the others. When it came, Dante held it for me as I put it on, then gently lifted my hair free. It was a casual, intimate gesture. I thought back to what both Nicole and Mrs. Weber had said about the way Dante looked at me. It was still hard for me to believe his words from earlier in the night, but maybe, just maybe, I should.

Chapter 18

Dante

I turned into the parking lot of the apartment complex, then pulled into my spot and killed the engine. Mia had been quiet on the drive home and I wondered what was going through her head. There was an awareness between us, a tension that hadn't been there before. We'd both acknowledged that we wanted more – thank God for that – and now it was like we were both holding our breath, on edge to see what would happen next.

I felt keyed up, my whole body tense. I looked over at Mia. She didn't seem nervous, but…

"You okay?" I reached over and ran my fingers over her arm. I wanted my hands on her in some way, felt an overwhelming need to touch her.

Mia turned to look at me, that sweet smile I loved so much on her face.

"Yeah, I'm okay. You alright?"

I'd been wrong – she was nervous. I could hear it in her voice. I smiled at her, ignoring the knots in my stomach and the steel pipe threatening to rip out the zipper of my jeans.

"I'm way better than just alright. Sit tight and I'll be around to help you down, okay?"

I stepped out of the truck and made my way around to Mia's door.

The thought of having my hands on her again, of sliding her body down mine as I lifted her out of the truck almost made me groan out loud. My rock-hard dick swelled even more. There would be no hiding the bulge in my pants from Mia. She was going to see it and feel it. I hoped she was ready for it. Thinking about Mia's eyes on my dick, her body brushing against it, had me gritting my teeth and forcing myself to calm the fuck down before I came in my pants.

I opened Mia's door and as she turned to me, I lifted her down. I set her on her feet, still holding her close to me. I could tell from her quick intake of breath that she had definitely felt my hard-on pushing at her. Thank God I hadn't gone commando tonight or the pattern of my zipper would be forever embedded in my dick.

Mia's eyes shot up to mine and in them I saw what I needed. Nerves, yes, but above all there was heat. Heat and longing and want. She was with me. I wasn't alone in this.

I pulled her closer and couldn't control the low groan that left me. I buried my face in her hair and ran my nose along her cheek. Mia's arms came around me as she shivered.

"I want to kiss you, Mia. I want to take your mouth and see if you're as sweet as I've dreamed."

I pressed my lips lightly at the juncture of her neck & shoulder and tasted her skin with the tip of my tongue. Her light scent and the feel of her soft skin under my lips made me feel off balance, like I was drunk on her.

Mia tightened her arms around me as her breath hitched and she shivered again.

"Then kiss me."

Her voice was husky and breathless, different than I'd ever heard it. Was this what she would sound like as she came? The thought of hearing her call out my name in that tone made my heart rate kick up another notch.

"Let's go upstairs." I reluctantly stepped back a little and reached up for Mia's hands around my neck. "Call me old fashioned but I don't want our first kiss to be in the parking lot where anyone could be watching us." I rested my lips on Mia's forehead in a light kiss. "And once I get my mouth on yours, I'm not going to want to stop."

I kept my eyes on Mia's as I backed away, still holding her hand, until she started after me. I kept her hand in mine as we crossed the lot and climbed the stairs. Those fucking stairs had never seemed so long. It took forever to get to the top. I steered us toward Mia's door and took the key she handed me to unlock the door. I pulled her inside, pulled the door closed behind us, and pushed Mia back against it as gently as I could. As Mia looked up at me, I put one hand on the door next to her head and threaded my other hand through her beautiful hair. I leaned into her, keeping my eyes pinned to hers as her hands came to rest on my hips. Neither of us said a word, just looked into each other's eyes, our lips a mere inch apart. Finally, Mia gave me what I'd been waiting for, a slight lift of her chin as if her mouth was seeking mine. I closed the short distance and settled my lips on Mia's.

Her lips were soft and warm and perfect under mine. I fought to keep the kiss light, brushing my mouth across Mia's lips when all I wanted was to dive in and claim her mouth completely. I pressed my lips against Mia's more firmly and tasted a hint of citrus from the sparkling water and lime she'd been drinking. Mia's lips parted slightly and I felt the tentative touch of the tip of her tongue on my bottom lip. She'd opened up for me, shown me that she wanted more, and I was ready to give it to her.

I couldn't hold back anymore as I slipped my tongue past Mia's lips and took what I'd needed for what felt like forever. I tilted my head to deepen the kiss even more and felt Mia's hands move from my arms as she slid them up and tightened her arms around my neck. She pressed herself closer and I slid my hand to her back to pull her into me as closely as I could. Our bodies were melded together, not a millimeter of space between us.

I lost time as our kiss went on, our mouths locked together, tongues dueling and tangling. Mia sucked lightly on my tongue and I groaned as she pressed her hips against the bulge in my crotch. I moved slightly, pushing my thigh between hers. She made a little sound and began slowly rubbing one thigh along the outside of mine. Her soft breasts felt fucking amazing pushed against my chest and I could feel the warmth of her arousal on my thigh. I slid my hand down to her leg and felt silky skin. I slipped my hand under her skirt, almost desperate to feel the heat and wetness of her arousal on my fingers.

Suddenly, I thought of waking up on my couch that morning with Mia sprawled on top of me and remembered thinking that I wanted to wake up that way every day. When I woke up again, she was gone. She'd left without waking me and I'd missed her presence more than I probably should have. Had it just been that morning? Things had changed so much so fast. I'd dodged a bullet when Mia had forgiven me for lying about tonight. I didn't want to rush her or make her have second thoughts. I never wanted to wake up and find her gone without a word again. As much as I wanted to feel Mia's wetness, to sink my fingers inside her and make her come, I needed to slow this down. I needed to know she was sure.

Chapter 19

Mia

*D*ante pulled away and I looked up at him in confusion.

"Mia, we have to stop." Dante's face was flushed. His breathing was ragged and his eyes as they met mine were hot and intense. Why was he stopping?

"Don't you want…" me? This? Had I read him wrong somehow?

"Oh, I want." Dante's low voice made me shiver. "I want to strip you out of those pretty clothes and see all of you. I want to touch and kiss and lick every inch. I want to eat your sweet pussy until you scream, to slide inside you and make you come on my dick again and again and again until you beg for mercy."

Thank God Dante was still holding me or I would have melted right on to the floor.

"But what I *need*…what I need is to know you're sure. I threw a lot at you tonight. I didn't plan to do any of this. You said yourself that you were overwhelmed. If we do this…"

Dante broke off as his cheek nuzzled mine, then he captured my lips in another slow, deep kiss, our tongues tangling, his hand firm on the back of my head. He drew back, sucking lightly on my bottom lip as he pulled away.

"*When* we do this, I need to know that you're with me a hundred percent. That I didn't rush you, that you had time to think."

As much as I hated to admit it, he was right.

"You're right. I know you are. I don't want to stop, but you're right. We should."

Dante nodded. "Okay." He took a deep breath and loosened his hold on me a little, then reached up to run his hand over my hair. "Okay,' he said again like he was settling himself down. "Can I see you tomorrow?"

I rubbed my hands slowly up and down his back, enjoying just touching him and being pressed against him. He'd stepped back a fraction but there was still no space between us. I loved the feel of him against me. With effort, I pulled my brain back to his question.

"Yes. I'm off so I have the whole day open."

Dante nodded again.

"Good, me too. Why don't you text me when you're up and we'll figure out a plan."

I agreed then Dante stepped back and just stood looking at me for a second. I wondered what he saw. I could feel that my cheeks were still flushed and my lips were swollen from our kisses. I knew my hair had to be a mess from his hands. Just as I thought that he reached up and smoothed his hand over my hair again. He shook his head and took another deep breath.

"I cannot fucking believe that I'm about to walk away from you and go to my own bed alone." Dante groaned and closed his eyes. "I've lost my mind."

For some reason his statement and the rampant frustration behind it made me smile. I put my hand on his chest and he opened his eyes to look at me.

"No, you haven't. You're being smart for both of us. This is the right thing to do right now. Even though it sucks."

Dante huffed out a laugh and his lips turned up in a rueful smile. "That it does."

He stepped close again and rested his forehead on mine. I closed my eyes and breathed in his scent, wanting to pull it into me to help me fill what was sure to be a lonely night ahead.

"It's only a few hours, right?" Dante said softly and I nodded.

"Okay." Dante said again and I felt him gather himself like he was preparing to step away. He kissed my forehead, then the tip off my nose, making me smile. I was still smiling when he murmured against my lips, "One more kiss."

I opened up for him and he slid his tongue inside my mouth, kissing me slowly and completely. Without thought, I slid my arms up to Dante's shoulders and fell into the kiss, fell into him. Much too soon Dante pulled back and rested his forehead on mine again.

"Damn, girl, you are dangerous."

We both had our eyes open and this close I could see the flecks of green and gray in Dante's dark eyes.

"Dream about me, okay?"

I couldn't help my smile. "I'm sure I will."

At that, Dante's lips met mine again for a quick peck then he pushed back away from me. The loss of his touch and heat was almost a physical pain. Dante gently but firmly set me out of the way and opened my door. He looked back at me as he stepped out.

"Good night, baby. I'll see you tomorrow. Lock the door behind me, okay?"

At my nod, Dante gave me one last look, his gaze burning into me, then quietly closed the door. I stepped forward to turn the locks and a few seconds later heard Dante's door open and close.

I stood for a minute still in a daze. Had this night really happened? A few short hours ago I'd believed that Dante saw me as a friend but certainly nothing more. I'd lost count of the times I'd told Meg exactly that. Now that was turned completely on its head. Could he really want me for more? If the kisses we'd shared tonight were any indication, the answer was a definite yes. And he'd called me baby, right? I shook my head at myself. Standing here wasn't going to get this figured out. Only time would do that.

I shot a quick text to Meg to let her know that the night had gone great and got a "you go girl" GIF and the message *Details tomorrow!* in return. Meg was out of town for work again but had made me swear that I would text her when I got home.

Thinking about seeing Dante again tomorrow, I turned off the light and headed to bed. I was sure I'd have no problem keeping my promise to Dante to dream of him.

Chapter 20

Dante

I heard Mia lock her door behind me and a few steps later, opened my own door and stepped inside.

I didn't even bother to hit the light, just leaned back against the door, unbuttoned and unzipped my jeans, and pulled out my aching dick that had been straining against the denim for hours.

I ran my hand from the base up over the head, groaning out loud and wishing it was Mia's soft little hand wrapped around me instead of my own. Thinking of Mia's hand on me, I tugged once, twice, three times. By the fourth tug I felt my balls draw up and then I was coming hard all over my hand and my shirt. I rode the wave, feeling my legs shake as it tore through me.

As it faded away, I leaned my head back against the door, closed my eyes, and felt my heart rate start to return to normal. I'd jacked off more in the few months since I'd met Mia than I had in the past two years. I was a normal guy and I enjoyed sex, but I'd never felt like I did when I was around Mia. Or hell, like I did when I even thought about Mia. I felt driven to claim her, to touch her and slide inside her and hear her say she was mine. It was primal, raw, and I really didn't give a fuck. I couldn't stop it even if I'd wanted to try. And I didn't. I'd been drawn to Mia since the first time I'd seen her when she ran from me like a scared little rabbit. And now she'd admitted that she wanted me, too.

I roused myself from my spot against the door, my thoughts continuing to swirl as I headed to the bathroom to clean up. The night had gone from a potential shit show when Mia had panicked at seeing Haven to the best-case scenario of Mia forgiving me for my dumbass move of lying to her and then showing me that she felt the pull between us, too. I was glad that my plan of taking it slow with Mia had been blown to hell. It probably wouldn't have lasted long anyway given that I could barely keep my hands off her. Walking away from her tonight had been like leaving a part of myself behind. It had taken all of my willpower to do it. Even then, it had only been the thought of how devasting it would be if Mia had second thoughts after we'd been together that had given me the strength to walk out her door.

I had the whole day with her tomorrow to solidify the connection between us and do my best to erase any doubts she may have about whether I was the guy for her. I desperately needed to do that because I didn't know if I could walk away from Mia again. I'd been with her in my dreams so many times. Hopefully tomorrow we would make those dreams a reality.

Chapter 21

Mia

I woke up the next morning still in a bit of a daze from everything that had happened the day and night before. If someone had told me that I would start the day by waking up on top of Dante on his couch and end the night with him pressing my body to his and his tongue in my mouth, I would have told them they must be smoking something. It was hard to believe that after weeks of telling myself that Dante couldn't possibly want me, that somehow, he did want me. And he also wanted to spend the day with me today.

I grabbed my phone from the charger on my bedside table and brought up a text message to Dante. I started and deleted and started again and deleted again, before finally settling on something simple.

Me: Good morning.

Three dots immediately started dancing. Dante must have had his phone in his hand already to reply so quickly.

Dante: Good morning, sunshine. Did you sleep well?

Me: I did. You?

Dante: Not great, but I enjoyed the dreams. Did you dream about me, too, like you promised?

I blushed at the implication that Dante had dreamed about me –

and enjoyed it – but responded right back.

Me: I did. And I enjoyed it, too.

I hit send before I could second guess. If Dante could be flirty, I could, too.

Dante: You know you just made me hard, right?

Wow, that was taking it up a level. The image that brought to mind made my blush burn brighter and my nipples start to tighten. I thought of Dante laying on his bed in nothing but boxer briefs, one arm bent behind his head, toned biceps and abs on display and an impressive bulge straining his briefs. My heart rate picked up and my panties grew damp.

Dante: Sorry, too much? Did I offend you?

Damn, while I'd been daydreaming, Dante had been waiting on a response, obviously thinking he'd screwed up.

Me: No! Not at all. Sorry it took me a minute. I was distracted by a really nice mental image.

There. Hopefully that would get us back on track and let Dante know that he wasn't going too fast for me. I knew he was worried about that and I didn't need to give him any more reason for doubt.

Dante: Yeah? I'd love to invite you over to my apartment to compare your mental image to reality, but…

Me: Tempting. Almost irresistible. But…?

Dante: But it's supposed to be a beautiful day and I was planning to ask if you'd be interested in going with me to the big vendor fair out at the fairgrounds. And if you come over to my apartment right now, I guarantee we won't be leaving again for quite a while.

I felt myself shiver as I read Dante's text. If he could make me this hot with just a few words, I was in trouble. I wanted to go knock on his door right this second, but I forced myself to keep my response light.

Me: Choices, choices…but yes, I'd love to spend a beautiful day with you out at the fairgrounds.

Dante: Dammit, I mean, great!!!

I laughed as the dots danced again.

Dante: Kidding! I'd love to spend the day with you. I always hit the vendor fair to grab basic stuff for the gym and it would be fun to wander around with you. You never know what you'll find.

Me: That sounds like a great way to spend the day.

Dante: Glad you think so. Meet you in maybe 20 minutes? We can grab breakfast on the way.

Twenty minutes? Had he never met a girl before?

Me: It's so cute that you think I can go from my bed to heading out the door in 20 minutes. Give me 45.

   Dante: Wait, you're still in bed?? Forget the vendor fair, I'll be right over.

   I didn't know anyone who made me laugh as much as Dante did. Not even Meg.

   Me: Goodbye, Dante. See you in 45 min.

   Dante: Damn, you're mean. But okay, see ya soon.

   I laughed again as I headed for the shower. I had a feeling this was going to be a day to remember.

~

   Hours later, as we headed home from the fairgrounds, I was glad I'd been right. I couldn't believe we'd spent the whole day at the vendor fair, but the hours had flown by.

   Dante had greeted me with a sweet, soft good morning kiss before we headed out in his truck. After a quick breakfast at a coffee shop near our apartment complex, we'd hit the highway for the thirty-minute drive out to the fairgrounds. We'd spent the whole day browsing through booth after booth, holding hands, just taking our time. Dante knew several of the vendors from his past trips, so we spent some time chatting with each of them while Dante purchased the various supplies he needed for the gym. We stopped at whichever booths caught our eye and ended up buying much more stuff than we intended. We made several trips back to Dante's truck to lock our purchases in the huge toolbox in the bed of his truck. I learned a lot about Dante, like the fact that he could not pass up a collection of old tools or vinyl albums without looking through them and that he put ketchup on his hot dogs. We had quite the debate about that since I'm firmly in the mustard and relish camp. I told him that might be a deal breaker, but he promised to overlook my habit of dipping my potato chips in mayo, so we called a truce on our food quirks. More importantly, I learned that he was incredibly patient when I was looking at something I was interested in, a great negotiator but fair in the final prices he agreed to, and he kept his sense of humor and fun when he was hot and tired and trying to make his way through a crowd.

   All-in-all, it was the perfect way to get to know each other better and I told Dante so on the drive back home.

   "Yeah? I agree." He glanced over at me with a smile as he drove. "I'm glad you think so, too."

   My arm rested on the center console, my left hand held in Dante's right, our fingers intertwined. Dante lifted my hand to his mouth and kissed it almost absently, then chuckled.

"I still can't believe you bought that ugly-ass lamp."

I'd seen the lamp tucked in the corner of a huge booth stuffed full of a little bit of everything. It had a bright pink swirly base and the lamp shade had a shimmer to it that reminded me of tinsel on a Christmas tree. I'd been looking for a small lamp for the table right inside my apartment door where I always set my keys when I came in. For some reason when I'd seen it, I'd just had to have it. It wasn't my normal style at all, but I was feeling adventurous today.

"Hey! Don't make fun of my lamp. It's beautiful!"

I frowned at Dante and tugged on my hand. Instead of letting go, he kissed my hand again.

"Sure it is, baby."

I rolled my eyes at his placating tone. "Now you're just humoring me. It's not my fault you don't know style when you see it."

"Well, if that's style, I definitely don't see it." Dante was holding back a laugh and knowing that made me want to smile, too. Instead, I sighed dramatically and pouted.

"Fine. The true visionaries are always mocked."

Now Dante did laugh, and I laughed along with him. I'd been momentarily nervous this morning about how things would be between us today. I'd wondered if we would feel awkward, if we'd both be unsure what to say or do. But it hadn't been that way at all. Dante and I just clicked together. In some ways it felt like we'd been together forever, but with the edge and anticipation of something new.

"I was gonna ask if you wanted to clean up and then go to dinner when we get back, but I think we're both kind of beat. What do you think about ordering pizza or Thai and kicking back on my couch that you like so much?"

"You had me at pizza or Thai, but throw in that awesome couch and I'm definitely in." Dante's couch was seriously the most comfortable one I'd ever sat on.

"Hey, I'm not above bribing you with my furniture if I have to."

We pulled into our parking lot a few minutes later and decided to leave our purchases locked up in the toolbox for the moment. They were safe and we didn't feel like lugging everything up the stairs. We agreed on pizza for dinner – we might as well make the day a complete diet disaster – and, after a quick kiss from Dante, I headed to my apartment to shower. I dried my hair the best I could in the time I was willing to give it and decided against make-up. Dante had seen me without it plenty of times and it apparently hadn't bothered him, so I wasn't going to obsess about it now.

Deciding what to wear made me pause for a minute. I felt weird putting on a fancy bra and panty set - we were just hanging out and having pizza. But I thought – I hoped – there was a really good chance that Dante would see everything I had on tonight, so I wanted to wear something nice. I finally settled on a light blue set with little flowers along the band of the bra and on one hip of the panties. It was a pretty color and my boobs and butt looked good in it. I slipped on a soft t-shirt, pulled on comfy shorts that looked good and showed off my legs, then locked up my apartment and walked across the landing to knock on Dante's door.

I heard a faint "come in" in response to my knock. I walked in as Dante was walking out of his bedroom, blanket in hand.

"Hey." Dante came closer and kissed the top of my head, the gesture so filled with affection that it made my heart swell a bit. "I bought this for you the other day. I thought if I ever got a chance to hang out with you again, you'd have it to wrap up in."

"Trying to keep me from stealing any more of your sweatshirts and ending up sleeping on top of you?"

At my teasing words the heat in Dante's eyes flared and he stepped closer. He met my eyes as he brought his hand up and lightly circled my throat. It was a dominant move and I felt my blood run faster at the touch. I knew that Dante could feel the way my pulse had sped up under his hand by the way his pupils widened and his eyes burned into mine.

"Any time you want to be on top of me, you just let me know."

I didn't make a sound as Dante leaned his head closer and then his lips closed on my mine. I brought my hands up to his sides and opened my mouth for him, craving the feel of his tongue on mine. He gave me what I wanted, stroking my tongue with his, then pulling back to nip at my bottom lip. He leaned back in, the tip of his tongue touching mine…

And the doorbell rang.

Dante groaned and rested his forehead on mine.

"Pizza's here, huh?" I ran my hands up and down Dante's sides, trying to soothe the frustration we were both feeling at the interruption.

Dante let out a breath, then gave me a quick kiss and stepped away.

"Better be the best fucking pizza we've ever had," he grumbled as he moved to the door.

⌒

The pizza was good as always and we ended up eating it sitting on the world's best couch while we watched part of a movie marathon of classic horror films on TV. They made me shudder as much as their cheesiness made me laugh and they were a great excuse to snuggle close to Dante.

We were on our second movie, pizza long gone, when we got into a silly debate about the special effects in the movie we were watching. I was practically sitting on Dante's lap at that point and he dumped me on my back on the couch, leaned over me and started tickling me.

I squirmed mightily under Dante as I laughed, but quickly said "No tickling! It makes me cough!"

Dante stopped immediately, looking down at me. He was leaning over me, a little sideways, my legs on either side of him. He braced himself on his hands on either side of me.

"It makes you cough?"

"Yeah, I know it's weird. But I laugh, then I start coughing and I can't stop."

"Hm. So no tickling. Okay. What about this?"

My shirt had ridden up a bit as Dante tickled me, leaving a strip of bare skin exposed. Dante leaned his head down and began slowly and softly pressing a string of kisses on the skin along the top of my shorts. He slid his hands up my sides, pushing my shirt up a little and exposing more skin to his soft kisses. The sensation of his lips on me made me catch my breath and my pulse picked up. Dante looked up at me and I could tell that he had felt my reaction. His eyes intense, he held my gaze as he lifted me slightly, slipped my shirt up over my head and tossed it aside. He moved up, still laying between my legs, but positioned so he could transfer his attention to the exposed skin along the top of my bra. He moved his hands up my ribcage, his thumbs brushing the skin just below my breasts. At his touch, my nipples hardened, and without thinking I arched my back a little to get closer to his mouth. I gripped Dante's biceps, needing something solid to hold on to. His mouth on the skin along the tops of my breasts, his hands on my body, felt so good, but it wasn't enough. He was so close to what I wanted, what I needed, but not close enough.

"Dante, please." I barely recognized my voice. It was rough and needy.

"Please what, baby?" The need I'd heard in my own voice was straining Dante's, too. He brushed his fingertips along one nipple over the surface of my bra and I couldn't stop a soft moan from escaping. "Is this what you need?"

It was but…it wasn't. I wanted Dante's mouth, his touch on my bare skin, was almost desperate for it. I couldn't believe how quickly I'd reached this point. I was a little embarrassed at my response, but there was no holding back.

I shook my head at Dante, letting him know I wanted more. I couldn't get the words out, but he understood. He reached up and slipped my bra strap off my shoulder, then gently pulled the cup of my bra down to expose my tight nipple. He dipped his head, his eyes holding mine until the last second, and closed his lips around my nipple. He flicked his tongue across it, and my back arched, pressing my body against his. The sensation of his lips and tongue on my nipple was so intense, it was like my whole being had centered right there. Dante lifted his head, moving over to pull my bra down on the other side and kiss and suck that nipple as he ran his fingertips over the other. It was like there was a direct connection between my nipples and my center. Every tug and touch on my breasts was echoed in the growing heat between my legs. I reached up and held Dante's head to me and felt my hips move up into his without thought. I could feel that my panties were soaked through. Dante groaned as I pressed my center against the bulge in his crotch. I felt his hands move underneath my back, then my bra slipped away and joined my shirt on the floor.

Dante lifted himself up a little and sat just looking at my bare breasts, wet and swollen from his mouth. A wave of shyness hit me as he stared. I moved to cover myself with my hands, but he caught them in one of his and held them, resting them on my stomach.

"You don't ever need to cover yourself around me. I love looking at you. You're so beautiful." Dante swallowed as he shifted his eyes up to mine. "I can't believe I'm the one who gets to see you like this."

"Take your shirt off, Dante. I want to see you, too."

Dante let go of my hands and I resisted the urge I still had to move them to cover my breasts. Dante reached back, grabbed his shirt and pulled it over his head. The minute his beautiful body was in view I forgot all about using my hands to do anything other than run them over his skin. I remembered how warm and smooth it was from the massages I'd given him. Now I could run my hands all over him like I'd wanted to then. I ran my hands across his chest, then down his sides and across his abs. I could feel Dante practically vibrating, like he was forcing himself to stay still under my hands. I moved my hands lower on his abs, coming dangerously close to the bulge in his shorts. He finally moved, grabbing both of my hands in his again.

Dante's eyes burned into mine and his cheeks were flushed.

"Mia, baby, I need to know what we're doing. If you're not ready for everything tonight, if you just want to play, I'm okay with that. I'll give you whatever you want. But I need to know what's okay, if I get to taste your sweet pussy and slide inside your softness and heat. If you're not ready, that's okay. I just need to know."

I could feel the tension in every muscle in his body. Yet I knew he was telling the truth. I knew if I told him I wasn't ready, he would wait. But that was the last thing that I wanted.

I met his eyes, wanting him to know I was sure of what I was about to say.

"I want everything, Dante. I'm ready."

Relief warred with heat in Dante's eyes as he reached down to scoop me up. I squeaked a little as he lifted me, the experience of being carried new to me.

Dante carried me into his bedroom without a word and laid me on his bed. He pulled off my shorts, then his. He joined me on the bed, pulling me under him, legs tangling with mine. He captured my mouth in a kiss and all conscious thought left my head as I ran my hands over the smooth skin of his back. The kiss went on and on, until the need for oxygen forced us apart. Dante's lips left mine and he began to move down my body, kissing, licking, and touching his way along. He reached the edge of my panties, dropping kisses from my hipbone along the edge to my belly, stopping just above my mound. He paused for a second, then dropped a soft, lingering kiss on my center. I could feel the heat of his breath on me through my panties and it was everything I could do not to shift my hips upward to get closer to his mouth.

"You're wet, baby." He looked up my body at me, eyes black as night and full of fire, voice low and tight.

"I am," I acknowledged, my voice matching Dante's.

"God, you smell amazing." Dante brushed the tip of his nose along my seam through my panties, then pressed his tongue against the fabric. I could feel the heat and wetness of his tongue and I couldn't hold back a soft moan. "I can't wait to taste you."

He slipped his fingers in the edge of my panties and my breath hitched. I'd never had a guy put his mouth…there. Neither of the guys I'd been with had been into it, although they were more than happy for me to have my mouth on them. I wanted Dante's mouth on me, was almost desperate for it, but that didn't stop me from being nervous.

Dante paused and looked up at me.

"Is this okay, Mia?"

I nodded but had to swallow hard before I could get words out.

"It is, but Dante, you don't have to."

"I want to. You have no idea how bad I want to. But only if you want it." Dante studied me for a second, then turned his head and pressed a soft kiss to my inner thigh. "Have you ever had this, baby? Has a man ever made you feel good this way?"

This time I couldn't force the words out. I shook my head and felt my face heat in embarrassment.

Dante closed his eyes for a couple seconds, and when he opened them the fire in them burned even hotter.

"Please let me, baby. I promise you I want this. I'll make you feel so good." Dante's voice was as hot as his eyes. His arms lay under my parted legs and his big hands gripped my hips from underneath. I could feel his breath on me and his light kisses on my center. I knew that if I said no, he'd move away no matter how badly he wanted it. I was still nervous. This was as intimate as you could get. But I wanted it and I trusted Dante.

I reached a hand down and smoothed it over Dante's head. His eyes still held mine and I nodded, giving him the answer we both wanted.

Dante turned his head and bit my thigh lightly, making me squeak, then pulled my panties down and off my body. He repositioned himself between my bent legs, gently pushing them wider apart. He just gazed at my center for few seconds, then dipped his head. At the first touch of his tongue on my clit, I knew that I wasn't going to last long. I was already so close and the feel of his mouth on me was incredible. He flattened his tongue and swiped firmly from my opening to my clit, then latched onto my clit and sucked. Sensation shot through me as my back arched up off the bed and I gasped for breath. Dante laid his arm across my hips to hold me in place and settled in, licking and sucking, bringing me to the brink of screaming in what seemed like mere seconds. I felt a touch at my opening and groaned out loud as Dante slipped a finger inside me. He stroked my inner walls and I could feel my body start to tighten, feel the tension start to build. I felt Dante slip a second finger inside me. The added pressure and the stroke of his fingers on that perfect spot had me straining against his firm hold on my hips. Panting, near desperate, I felt Dante's lips close around my clit again and I was gone. My pussy clenched and sensation streaked through me. Wave after wave hit me until I thought I might pass out. My legs shook and my heart rate soared. I knew I was making desperate sounds, saying Dante's name and God knows what else, but I couldn't stop. Finally, I slowly, slowly started to float back to earth, shuddering as I felt Dante's tongue move across me one last time and his fingers gently pull out of my body.

Dante lay for a minute with his head resting on my mound, nuzzled his face on my belly, then kissed his way slowly up my body again. He sat up, resting back on his heels, my open thighs draped over his. He looked at me, taking in my dazed expression and his face broke into a huge grin.

"Good, baby?" He sounded happy and very proud of himself. Justifiably so, but I couldn't help teasing him a little.

"Eh, it was fine." I shrugged and tried to keep a straight face, but couldn't help joining in when Dante laughed, his eyes lighting up with amusement and something that looked like pure happiness.

"Only fine, huh?"

Dante leaned forward, his hands on either side of me and the big, hard, bulge in his briefs pressed firmly against my still wet and sensitive center. I caught my breath at the pressure and moaned when Dante began to move his hips back and forth slowly, thrusting against me and retreating. There was only one thin layer of fabric preventing him from rubbing directly against me skin-on-skin, from slipping inside me, and my pussy clenched and grew wetter at the thought.

"Ready to try for better than fine?"

"Yes." My voice was barely above a whisper, but that was all I could get out. "Please."

Dante moved away and I made a little sound of protest, but then realized he was just reaching for the drawer of his bedside table. I saw a square condom wrapper in his hand, then Dante was removing his briefs and moving back in between my legs. He quickly rolled the condom on and my first look at his long, beautiful, flushed dick made my breath hitch. Then Dante leaned forward, positioned himself right against my opening, and paused, looking at me intently.

"Are you sure, Mia? Sure you want this with me?"

I met Dante's eyes, the vulnerability I saw there making my heart squeeze. I held his gaze as I answered, hoping he could see how right this felt to me.

"I'm a hundred percent sure, Dante. I want this. I want you."

I thought of the glimpse I'd had of him and how large he felt notched against me.

"It's been a while for me, so maybe go slow, okay?"

Dante's eyes flared again, and he leaned forward, resting his lips against mine.

"Anything you need."

He captured my mouth in a slow kiss, then leaned back and began to slowly push inside me. Jaw clenched, he pulled back a little, then pushed a little further inside, repeating the pattern until he was fully seated inside me, his balls pressed firmly against my butt. I felt stretched and full, but in the best possible way. Dante moved to lay over me, supporting most of his weight on his forearms. He leaned in for another long kiss as I ran my hands over the smooth skin of his sides and back. He nudged my chin up with his cheek and kissed along my neck, then shifted down a little to capture one of my nipples in his mouth. He kept his hips still, giving me time to adjust to having him filling me. As Dante sucked on first one nipple, then the other, the need to feel him move inside me built and built until I couldn't take it anymore. I gripped his hips and began to move mine, drawing a groan from Dante. He moved his mouth back to my neck and began moving his hips in rhythm with mine. I wrapped my arms around his neck and spread my legs a little wider, changing the angle and feeling Dante slip a little deeper.

Dante groaned again into my neck. "Fuck, baby. You feel so good."

He sat up and put his hands under me, lifting and tilting my pelvis. The change in angle had Dante hitting the perfect spot inside me with every thrust of his hips and I felt the tension in me wind tighter and tighter. I gripped Dante's forearms, digging my nails in a little, as he pushed me closer and closer to the edge.

"Dante." I heard the pleading note in my voice. I was close, so close, but I needed...I needed...

Dante leaned into me, slipping his hand behind my lower back, pressing my body as close to his as it could be. With each thrust of his hips his dick dragged across my clit with the perfect friction, the perfect pressure...

I catapulted off the edge of the earth, the pleasure so intense it was almost painful. My whole body shook as my pussy clenched again and again on Dante's dick as it pistoned in and out of me. I could hear a keening sound and knew it was me but had no power to stop it. I knew I was raking my nails down Dante's back as the waves of pleasure slammed into me again and again. My heart pounded and my skin felt electrified. The waves had barely started to recede when

Dante changed position again, sitting up and pulling my right leg up to rest on his shoulder. The position opened me more fully to him and I couldn't believe how quickly the tension began to build again. Almost before I could catch my breath, I reached the peak and broke apart again. Seconds later I felt Dante tense, then heard him groan as he pressed himself inside me and came.

As I spiraled down slowly, I felt Dante shift us slightly to the side, keeping most of his weight off me. He was still inside me and we lay there for a few minutes, our breathing finally slowing to normal. Dante stirred, slipping out of the bed and into the adjoining bathroom. I heard water running, then Dante returned to the bed, pulling me close, my head on his shoulder, one leg across his.

He smoothed his hand over my shoulder and down to my hip and pressed a kiss on the top of my head.

"You okay?" He sounded relaxed and a little sleepy.

"I'm much better than okay. You?" I ran my hand across his chest and abs, feeling warm and happy and peaceful.

"Never better. Will you stay with me tonight?"

"Yes, I'll stay."

"Good." Dante pulled me closer and kissed the top of my head again. I felt his body relax a few seconds later and knew that he'd fallen asleep. I reached down and grabbed the sheet we'd all but kicked off the bed. Pulling it over us, I settled back into Dante's side and drifted off.

Chapter 22

Dante

For the second time in three days, I woke up with Mia draped across me. Even better, today we were both naked in my bed. As it had the first time I'd woken with Mia, the thought filled my mind that I wanted to start every day for the rest of my life just like this.

I was in love with Mia. I didn't even try to fight it, wouldn't even if I could. She'd slipped into my life with her quiet voice and her sweet smiles and taken over my heart and soul. Her soft touch both soothed me and set my body on fire.

I'd never been in this deep with a woman before. I'd dated other girls and spent two years with Haven and had never even come close to scratching the surface of what I had with Mia. Mia and I had barely even gotten started and already I knew I'd be completely destroyed if she ever walked away from me. I'd do everything in my power to make sure that never happened.

I knew I was way ahead of Mia in the intensity of my feelings for her. But I also knew that she felt something for me, or she wouldn't have slept with me. She wasn't the kind of woman who had casual sex. I thought back to the fact that she apparently hadn't been with anyone since she'd moved here – two years, she'd said. I couldn't believe she hadn't had opportunities. I'd seen the way men looked at her at the pub and again at the event last night. She seemed oblivious to her own appeal, but there were plenty of men around who weren't. She'd clearly been with at least one guy before, although I really, really didn't want to know details. I would have been shocked if she hadn't been with someone, but the thought of some other man's hands on her made me want to punch a wall. Whoever it was, he hadn't treated her right. The selfish part of me was glad. When she'd said she hadn't had oral sex before and I realized that somehow I was the lucky one who got to be the first – and I hoped to God, only – one to ever do that for her, the feeling that had overwhelmed me had been intense. To have that first with her was much more than I could have hoped for.

Remembering Mia's taste and scent I felt my dick stir to life. I swore I reverted to my teenage years when it came to Mia, popping a boner at the mere thought of the girl I liked. It didn't help that her warm, soft, naked body was draped across me. As much as I wanted to wake Mia up slowly and sweetly as I slipped into her body, I also wanted to take it a little slow. We'd gone warp speed through the past two days, and I needed to give Mia some time to catch up to what I was feeling. And although I hated to let the real world intrude, I was on the schedule to open the gym today. A quick glance at the clock told me I had just enough time if I got moving. I knew Mia didn't have to work until later today, so I could let her sleep a little longer. I pulled myself away from her as gently as I could and slipped out of the bed. I gave myself a minute to appreciate the beautiful sight of Mia naked in my bed, then turned and headed for the shower.

Fifteen minutes later, I walked back into the bedroom. I chuckled when I heard Mia snoring softly. I'd be teasing her about that later for sure, but for now I just wanted to let her know that I was leaving.

I sat next to Mia on the bed and shook her gently. "Mia, sweetheart. Wake up, baby."

Mia surfaced slowly, blinking her eyes as she turned her head and focused on me.

"Morning." The sleepy smile that lit up her face made me want to crawl right back in bed with her.

"Morning, sweetheart. I'm sorry to wake you up. I just wanted to let you know that I'm leaving. Sleep as long as you want, unless you need to get up for work."

Mia looked at the clock on my bedside table. "I still have about an hour. But I can go if you're leaving."

I shook my head as I leaned forward to kiss her cheek. "You can stay right here. Snuggle up and go back to sleep for a bit. I like the thought of you warm and naked in my bed."

Mia blushed but gave in. I told her I'd leave her my spare key so she could lock the door when she left. She was having dinner with Meg after work since Meg was finally back in town from all her travels, but Mia agreed to text me when she got home so I could see her. I felt a little pathetic, but I knew I didn't want to end the day without seeing Mia for at least a few minutes. And she seemed happy about it, so it was all good.

I had an easy drive to the gym, and I was hoping for a good day. We usually had a good flow of people in and out on Mondays, not crazy like Saturdays and not slow like Fridays.

My hopes for a smooth day faded before I even got into the gym. I heard a sound behind me as I unlocked the door and turned around to see Pete standing a few feet away. He looked bad, his clothes wrinkled like he'd slept in them, his hair disheveled and his eyes…his eyes looked kind of crazy. For the first time, I wondered if he might be on something.

"What are you doing here, Pete?" I kept my voice firm and calm, though I was still pissed at him for telling Silas March that he could get me to fight again. March had backed off graciously but just from my short talk with him I'd gotten the impression that he was not someone to fuck around with.

Pete came forward a few steps and I turned to face him fully. He was agitated, even more twitchy than usual, and I wanted to be ready for whatever he might do.

"You know why I'm here." Pete's voice was raspy and tense. "You told Silas March that you're not going to fight again."

"That's right." I kept my arms and body loose, ready in case Pete came at me. He wouldn't normally, but as wound up as he was, he just might. "That's the same thing I've told you every time you asked me. Why were you telling him something different?"

Pete rushed forward a few steps, but stopped short when I held up a hand.

"You have to fight! It's just one fucking fight. You stay in shape; you train all the time. Why won't you do it?"

Pete's eyes were wild and he repeatedly clenched his hands into fists at his sides.

"I train, I stay in shape, but I'm not in fighting shape, Pete. Even if I was, that's not the point. Why do you care so much if I fight again?"

"Because I need the fucking money! I need the money March was going to pay me for getting you to fight! We're not all fucking million-aires!"

Behind Pete, I could see Dev approaching quietly from the parking lot. I met his eyes and nodded just a little, letting him know that I had things under control. He stopped a few feet behind Pete, ready to help if needed, but staying out of it for now.

"What do you need the money for, Pete? What's so important?"

Pete shook his head violently as if he hadn't even heard my question. He was pacing back and forth, shoving both hands through his hair.

"Just do it! Just fucking agree to fight! Do it, Dante!" he shouted.

Still keeping my voice calm, I gave Pete the answer I knew he didn't want to hear. "That's not going to happen, Pete. I'm not going to fight."

Pete suddenly froze where he stood, both hands clutching his hair. He stared at me, his eyes wilder than before.

"You'll be sorry you said that." His whisper and his stillness were almost eerie given the frantic energy of the moments before. "You'll be sorry."

He stepped back, then started as he caught sight of Dev. He broke into a run, scrambling away as if he thought we were chasing him.

I stepped inside the gym, Dev close behind me, and re-locked the door.

"What. The fuck. Was that." Dev looked back out through the gym door in the direction Pete had run, shaking his head.

I headed toward the break room, Dev following me.

"Silas March must have told Pete that he talked to me Saturday and I shut him down. Pete was freaking out. You heard him yelling about the money?"

"Yeah, I heard it. I think the neighbors three doors down heard it."

I stepped into the break room, flipping on the light. I stowed my stuff in my locker and turned to face Dev. He stood in the doorway, hands on his hips, concern clear on his face.

"Do you think he'll be a problem? He looked like he might be on something."

I crossed my arms over my chest and leaned my hip on the corner of the break room table. "I don't think so. He was definitely pissed, but he's always twitchy."

Dev eyebrows rose as he continued to look at me. "He was more than twitchy, Dante. He was coming out of his skin. And he clearly meant that 'you'll be sorry' bullshit as a threat."

"Yeah, he was pretty agitated, even for him." I reached a hand up and rubbed the back of my neck, the muscles there suddenly tense. "He'll cool down. I'll try to find him later, see if I can get him to tell me what the hell he needs money for and clear this shit up."

Dev looked doubtful, but he dropped his hands from his hips and stepped back as if he was going to head to the office. "Alright, but watch your back. Desperate people do crazy things."

Before I could respond to that, it hit me that Dev shouldn't even be there yet. He usually didn't come in until an hour or two after opening on Mondays.

I stopped him before he could walk away.

"Hey, not that I wasn't happy you were here for back-up if needed, but what are you doing here so early? New client coming in or something?"

Dev stopped in the hallway, hands back on his hips. His head dropped forward and he didn't say anything for a few seconds. When he raised his head and met my eyes, he looked a little defeated, a little resigned.

"Nicole is moving out today. We talked yesterday. It's just not going to work between us. She has friends coming over this morning to help. It was clear she didn't want me around, so I got out of the way." He shook his head and reached up to run a hand over his beard as he often did when he was thinking. "I should have known it." He blew out a breath, meeting my eyes again. "I did know it, even as I was moving her in. She knew it, too. We should have just called it then."

I couldn't disagree. I'd been surprised when Dev had said that he'd asked Nicole to move in with him. They disagreed on just about everything. It seemed like living together would make that worse not better, but who was I to say? I hadn't said it then and I wasn't going to say it now.

"I'm sorry, man. Sorry it didn't work out." I knew Nicole wasn't Dev's soul mate, but she was a good person and ending a relationship was never easy.

"Yeah, thanks. It's for the best." Dev straightened up, like he was done with the conversation and ready to move on. He grinned suddenly. "And it worked out for you, since you ended up with Mia." He eyed me curiously. "You did end up with her, right?"

Reading between the lines, I knew he was asking me if I'd gotten with Mia yet. I wasn't giving details, but I let the grin take over my face as I responded, "Yeah, I ended up with her."

Dev stepped forward, holding out a fist. "Good for you, man. She's a good one." I bumped his fist with mine. Turning around, he headed for the break room door again. "At least this relationship shit is working out for someone."

Chapter 23

Mia

*T*hank God for slow Mondays.

I'd gotten to work fine, even remembering to leave myself extra time to take the bus since Meg was picking me up tonight for dinner. My brain was so scrambled I was half surprised I'd even remembered. I typically worked on the schedule and other administrative things on Mondays because the number of people checking in and checking out was usually manageable by whichever front desk team members were working. I was in the office right behind the front desk, always available to lend a hand if needed, but more often than not on Mondays I had most of my shift to do other things.

The distractions today didn't come from the front desk, they came from my weekend with Dante. Images from the sponsor event, the vendor fair and, most of all, our incredible night together kept flipping through my head like a slide show I couldn't turn off. One minute I'd be working on the schedule, the next I'd be staring into space remembering the feel of Dante over me, his kisses and touches, the way he'd used his hands, his lips, his tongue – God, his tongue – on me. Blushing, I'd shake myself, get back to work for a while, then find myself staring off into space again.

After repeating the cycle for the third time in less than an hour, I sighed and stood up. The team members out front could always buzz

143

me if they needed anything, but maybe I'd just go check. I needed to move around a little and try to find a way to re-focus.

Stepping out of the office, I greeted the team members, Jackie and Rachel, who were working the desk that shift.

"Hey, ladies. How's it going? Everything good?" I hadn't heard a peep from either of them, so I assumed they'd say that everything was fine.

Instead, they exchanged a look, then Jackie surprised me by saying, "Well, we're not sure."

Jackie had worked at the hotel for nearly a year and was as steady as they came. For her to be concerned, something really must be off.

My brain already sorting through possibilities, I responded "Okay, what's up?"

Jackie walked over to one of the computer terminals and motioned me to come over. Once I stood next to her, she started clicking back and forth between screens in our registration system seemingly at random. I had no idea what the heck she was doing.

Jackie spoke quietly, adding to my confusion. "Act like I'm showing you something on the monitor. See, look at this," she said pointing at a zip code that looked perfectly fine.

I did as she asked, but questioned, "Ok, I'm looking but Jackie, what on earth is going on?"

"Don't look right now, but there's a man near the bar who's been giving us the creeps. I'll tell you when to look. He's wearing a blue shirt and acting like he's reading one of the free copies of the paper that's always around. He's sitting kind of over by the water wall. Okay, look, look!"

I scanned the lobby quickly and located a man fitting Jackie's description. He wasn't hard to find as he didn't look like our typical guest. The blue shirt he was wearing was badly wrinkled and his stringy hair hung down past the collar. He sat in one of the armchairs by the wall of water near the huge bar that dominated that part of the lobby. Though I could see the paper sitting on his lap, at the moment he was looking at his phone with a frown, his legs bouncing a mile a minute. Tearing my gaze away before he caught me looking, I focused back on the monitor and pointed at a random room number.

"Okay, I see him. What about him?"

"Like I said, he's giving me and Rachel the creeps. He keeps watching us. Like he holds the paper up like he's reading it, but if you look right at him you can tell he's watching the desk."

"Alright, that does sound a little weird." Rachel hung up the phone from helping a guest and I called her over to join us. No longer making the pretense of looking at the monitor, I just focused on her and Jackie. If the man happened to look over, or if he really was watching us, all he would see was three staff members talking. There was no way he could hear us from where he sat.

"How long has he been sitting there?" Jackie and Rachel looked at each other, then Rachel shrugged.

"Maybe an hour?"

"Has he done anything other than sit there, check his phone, pretend to read the paper, and stare at you?"

They both shook their heads. "No, that's it," Jackie said. "It's just the way he watches us is creepy."

"Yeah, it would creep me out, too. Unfortunately, if that's all he's done, I'm not sure there's anything we can do. For all we know, he could be meeting someone at the bar and they're running really late and that's making him nervous. He could be watching the two pretty women working at the front desk to take his mind off it." Out of the corner of my eye now I could see that he was definitely focused on the desk. He was staring openly, not even acting like he was reading the paper. Straightening my shoulders, I made a decision. "I'll notify security just to keep an eye out for him. He technically isn't doing anything wrong, so I'm sure they won't approach him, but at least they'll be aware that we have a concern. Does that sound okay? And you let me know if he does anything else or if anyone joins him."

Rachel and Jackie agreed, and I looked over my shoulder at the man as I returned to the office. His gaze touched mine for just a second. He was focused directly on me, his eyes intense and unfriendly. I shivered as I sat down at the desk to make the call to our security office. I didn't know what business, if any, the man had with the hotel, but I sincerely hoped he would move along soon.

About an hour later, Rachel stuck her head in the office to let me know that the man had left. No one had ever joined him and security, as expected, hadn't approached him. He'd just gotten up and walked out. Glad that he was gone, I thanked Rachel, shook my head at some of the strange people we encountered, and focused my mind back on paperwork.

～

The rest of the shift was quiet. When it was time to go, I waved goodbye to Jackie and Rachel as they headed to the employee parking garage and I headed to the front entrance where Meg was picking me up. I stepped out the doors, had about a minute to chat with the valet and bellman, and Meg zoomed up in her little sports car.

I climbed in the passenger side, Meg already chattering away at me.

"Hey, girl! I have missed the crap out of you. We have so much to catch up on!"

Meg looked perfect, as always. She was always so put together. Luckily, I'd had time to change out of my uniform into jeans and a cute sweater, but no matter what I always felt like the frumpy friend when I was with Meg. I knew that she didn't care, though. She was only judgmental about herself, not others.

"I missed you, too. We do have a lot to catch up on." I settled in my seat as Meg pulled out of the hotel driveway and threaded her way through traffic. My shift had ended at 7pm so thankfully the traffic had died down somewhat from rush hour. "You've been traveling so much. Do you get to stay home for a while?"

"I should, at least as long as that loser, Mike, doesn't come up with some reason that he just has to stay in town again." I could tell from her tone that Meg was rolling her eyes. She glanced over at me quickly, then focused back on the traffic. "I'm sorry I ever said you should date him. I never realized he was such a whiny baby until we ended up on the same team."

"Definitely a bullet dodged, then. Was the trip good at least?"

Meg filled me in on the project she'd just completed with her most recent client. She was a management consultant and traveled all over the country working with big companies on everything from strategic planning to performance improvement to leadership development. I was in awe of the extent of Meg's expertise and skills, but she never seemed satisfied. Listening to Meg talk about her work was always interesting and she always had a funny story or two to tell about her client or the trip.

Before I knew it, we were pulling into the lot behind a small Italian restaurant we both loved. Once we were seated and had ordered, Meg leaned toward me across the table and I knew the questions were about to start.

"Okay, Meems, enough about my job. What's going on with that hot boxer you've been spending time with? Spill it all, girl. Every dirty little detail."

I blushed, thinking about the fact that for probably the first time, I actually had some dirty-ish details to share. Not that I was going to get graphic, but still...

"Ooo, she's blushing! Come on, Mia. Is he amazing or what?" If Meg leaned any farther toward me, she was going to be climbing on the table.

Still feeling myself blushing, I nodded. "He's amazing. Really, really, in every way you can imagine, amazing."

Meg sat back in the booth seat, a huge grin on her face. "Does that mean what I think it does? Have you...?"

I nodded again and couldn't help smiling myself. "We have. And yeah, amazing covers that, too."

"Score!" Mia raised her hands in the air like she'd just won a prize, or like I had, I suppose. "Hallelujah, the dry spell is over. I was beginning to worry that all of your parts wouldn't work anymore."

I laughed but shushed Meg at the same time. No one seemed to be paying any attention to us, but the restaurant was small, and you never knew who might overhear what.

"You don't need to worry. Everything works just fine. And boy, was it worth the wait."

Meg leaned forward again, still smiling. "I am so happy for you, Meems. You really deserve a great guy. I told you he was into you. He was projecting it in waves that night at the pub."

I wasn't sure about all that, but Meg had definitely called it. There was no denying that she'd been telling me nonstop that Dante was interested in me, even as I'd insisted that he wasn't. I held up my hands in surrender.

"You were right. I admit it. This is one time I don't mind hearing, 'I told you so.'"

I paused for a minute as our server brought our food and refilled our water glasses, then launched into everything that had happened in the week that Meg had been gone. I'd already filled her in on some of the details via text, but I filled in the blanks from Saturday and told her about the great time Dante and I had had at the vendor fair Sunday. I glossed over the details of our night together – Meg knew better than to expect explicit details, although she'd teased me about sharing them – telling her just enough to let her know that Dante had taken very good care of me. As I was talking, I realized I needed some details from her, too. I took a sip of my wine, then turned the focus on her.

"Now it's your turn. Tell me about this Aaron guy." Before she'd left on this last work trip, Meg had gone out for drinks with a man she'd met a few weeks before that. He worked for a local firm she'd consulted with recently. She and Aaron had talked, and apparently flirted, a number of times while she was consulting with his company. A few days after the consulting engagement was over, Aaron had contacted Meg to ask her out. As Meg had described him, he sounded like a perfect fit for her type – tall, dark, handsome, and corporate.

"Okay, I'll start with the best part and back up from there." Meg settled back in her seat and pulled her phone out of her purse. "Get this - he surprised me while I was in Dallas this week. We were texting back and forth one evening and he was describing the incredible view from the rooftop bar he was at. Finally he sent me this..." Meg turned her phone around so I could see a beautiful view of a city at night, with the text message "Join me?" below it.

"I could tell from the view that he was at the rooftop bar of the hotel where I was staying. I immediately headed for the elevator. When I stepped out, he was standing right there, waiting with a glass of wine for me. He'd paid attention on our first date – our only date – and knew what wine to order for me. He'd known then that we were going to be in Dallas at the same time, but didn't tell me because he wanted to surprise me." Meg looked down at the text message on her phone, then looked at me again. Her eyes were shining and for the first time in a while, she looked happy. "It's the most romantic thing anyone has ever done for me."

I couldn't help but agree. "That's pretty impressive. I can't say I've ever had anyone follow me halfway across the country."

Meg grinned suddenly and her usual, sassy self reappeared. "So of course, I invited him to spend the night with me. I'll just say it was very good night." Meg finished her current glass of wine and set the glass aside. "He had a flight back home the next morning. We've texted a few times and we're having dinner Wednesday night."

I leaned forward, studying Meg's face closely. She seemed like she was into Aaron, but there was something else that I couldn't put my finger on. I decided to ask her straight out.

"So how do you feel about him? He seems into you, tracking you down like that while you were both in Dallas."

"I like him." Meg held up her hand and extended her fingers one by one as she went on. "He's smart, he's hot, he's loaded, he's great in bed, and did I mention he's hot?" She raised her hand, showing me her fingers and thumb spread wide. "What's not to like?"

Meg was smiling and saying all the right things, but...

Still unconvinced, I decided to voice my concern. "But...?"

Meg shook her head. "No buts. Not that he doesn't have a nice one of those, too." She reached for her wine glass again, realized it was empty, and set it back down. "It's all good, Mia, really. Be happy for me."

"I am, Mik." I didn't use Meg's childhood nickname as much as she used mine, but sometimes it slipped out. Hers was based on her initials – MIK. I teased Meg that mine was based on her being too lazy to say all two syllables of my name. I reached across the table and grabbed her hand. "I am happy. It just seems like there's something more."

Meg shrugged and smiled again. She squeezed my hand, then let go. "It's all good, Meems. I promise."

Giving up, I smiled back. "Well, he sounds amazing. He's not good enough for you, because no one is, but he sounds like he's close."

We switched to other topics and headed out soon after that. Meg dropped me off at my apartment with promises to text me after her date with Aaron on Wednesday.

I started up the stairs, thinking ahead to seeing Dante. I'd promised to text him when I got home, so as soon as I stepped inside the door and kicked of my shoes, I dug my phone out of my purse.

Me: Hey, I'm home.

Dante's reply popped right up.

Dante: B there in 2 min

Seeing Dante's reply I hustled to the bathroom to brush my teeth just in case he kissed me, which I really hoped he did. I heard a thump at the door as I came back down the hall. It was a weird sound, not exactly a knock. The reason became clear when I opened the door and saw Dante standing there, his arms full of my purchases from the vendor fair.

"Oh wow, come in. Just dump everything...um...on the kitchen table for now."

Dante walked past me, leaning in to give me a quick kiss on his way into the kitchen. He carefully set everything on the kitchen table and stepped back. I eyed the pile with both dismay and amusement.

"What the hell did I buy? Are you sure that's all mine?"

Dante stepped closer, pulling me into his arms.

"Afraid so, baby. All yours, just like me."

Before I could process what Dante said, he leaned his head down and captured my mouth with his, his lips warm and soft on mine. He pressed a little harder and I opened up for him, wrapping my arms around him as he deepened the kiss. After a minute, he pulled back, dropping soft kisses on my lips before raising his head.

"Hi."

His voice was a little husky and his beautiful smile made me smile in return.

"Hi, yourself."

Dante dipped in for another quick kiss before releasing me and taking a half step back. He looked down at the pile of items on the table again.

"Do you want help putting all of this away?"

I looked at it, thinking, then shook my head.

"Thanks, but no. I don't even remember what half of it is right now." Spotting the lamp I'd liked so much, I dug it out. "I know exactly where this goes though."

I carried it over to the small table that sat just inside my door. Moving my keys that were sitting there a little to the side, I set the lamp down, then leaned down to plug it in. I felt Dante move up behind me as I turned it on. As his arms circled me again, I leaned back into his chest. "There." I nodded in satisfaction. "It's perfect."

I felt Dante's chest rumble against my back as he chuckled. "As long as you like it, that's what matters."

"You just can't admit it's gorgeous."

"Huh-uh." Dante pulled my hair back gently and began kissing me softly on the neck. "You're gorgeous."

I titled my head to give him better access and leaned more of my weight back into him, pressing myself against him. My breath caught in my lungs as his hands slid up my body to cup my breasts. He squeezed them lightly and I arched my back a little to push them into his hands.

I felt Dante's warm breath on my ear. "Damn, baby, I'm sorry. I didn't mean to start all this. I just can't keep my hands off you. I'll stop if you want me to." He captured my earlobe between his lips, sucking lightly and making me shiver.

"No, don't stop." I turned in Dante's arms and met his eyes. They were full of fire and need, all for me. "I don't want to stop." I pulled Dante's mouth to mine and slipped my tongue inside as he parted his lips for me, letting me take the lead. Wherever shy Mia had gone, there was no sign of her tonight.

After a minute, I broke the kiss and still holding Dante's hand, turned down the hallway toward my bedroom. I flipped on the light as we walked in, then stopped at the side of the bed and faced Dante. I slid my hands up his body as his eyes burned into mine. He framed my face in his hands.

"Are you sure about this, Mia?" His voice was strained with need. Despite that, as always, he was thinking of me first.

"Yes, I'm sure. I want you inside me, Dante."

Dante's eyes closed and I felt his quick intake of breath. "Fuck, baby. What you do to me." He opened his eyes and his smile made my heart stutter. "My girl should always get what she wants."

I raised my arms as he pulled my sweater over my head, then he lowered me to the bed and pulled my jeans down my legs. I raised up on my elbows to watch him strip off his shirt and jeans. I watched as he pulled two condoms from the pocket of his jeans and tossed them on the bedside table.

Looking back at him, I raised my eyebrows. "Cocky much?"

Grinning, he shook his head. "Hopeful. Very hopeful."

Smiling, I looked down Dante's body and my eyes caught on the impressive bulge in his boxer briefs. I stared, remembering how good he'd felt inside me, and felt myself grow wetter between my legs.

I couldn't stop my blush as I laid down and reached my arms up to Dante. "Come here."

Dante lowered himself over me, careful to keep most of his weight off me. As I ran my hands over his back, he kissed me under my jaw, biting my earlobe softly, and kissing my neck. He made his way down my chest to the edge of my bra, then I felt the clasp loosen and my bra slipped away. Without conscious thought I moved my hands up to hold Dante's head to me as he licked and nibbled and sucked my nipples and breasts. He lay between my legs and I arched up into him. He tugged hard on one nipple with his teeth and the sensation shot directly to my center. I whimpered as I began rocking my hips against Dante's hardness. Dante groaned and moved his hand down my body, slipping his hand inside my panties and sliding two fingers inside me. I gasped and grabbed his biceps, needing an anchor to keep from flying off the bed. It was too much...and not enough at the same time.

"Please, Dante. I need you inside me."

Without a word, Dante leaned down, kissed my belly and slipped my panties off my body. He pulled his briefs off and reached for a condom, ripping it open and quickly rolling it on. He moved back between my legs and paused with his tip just barely resting at my entrance.

He still didn't speak, just looked down at me, his question clear in his eyes.

I nodded and let him see the need written clearly on my face. "I'm ready."

Leaning down to kiss me, Dante pushed slowly but firmly into me, my body accepting him more easily than it had the night before.

He moved in and out of me, his rhythm steady. I moved my hips with him, meeting each thrust. Soon Dante's breathing picked up and I felt him swell even bigger inside me. He picked up his pace, holding himself up on his forearms as his thrusts came harder and faster, slamming into me again and again. I felt the tension coil tighter and tighter inside me and I cried out as I came hard, my pussy clenching tight on Dante. He didn't let up, didn't slow his pace, just continued to piston in and out of me relentlessly. I held on, digging my nails into Dante's shoulders as the pressure built again. I whimpered and spread my legs wider, trying to let Dante deeper inside me, so close to flying again. Dante slipped a hand between us and pressed directly on my clit. I felt the tension snap and fell over the edge.

"That's right, come for me, baby. Fuck, you're so tight. God, Mia."

I felt Dante jerk inside me, then he was coming, jaw clenched, muscles tight, still thrusting in and out of me. His movements finally slowed, and his head dropped forward. I could feel his arms shake as he held his weight off me. He raised his head and started to say something, then stopped. He leaned down to kiss my forehead, then lifted himself off me and left the room. He reappeared a few minutes later and crawled into bed with me. His body was tense, and he still hadn't said a word, but he seemed to relax a little when I snuggled up next to him.

Well, if he wasn't going to say anything, I was. My head resting on his chest, I looked up at him, but he wasn't meeting my eyes.

"Dante, what's wrong?"

He smoothed his hand over my hair, and I felt him swallow. "Do I need to apologize?"

Apologize? For what?

I changed position, rolling over so I could stack my hands on Dante's chest and rest my chin on them, looking directly at him.

Frowning a little, I asked my question out loud. "What do you think you need to apologize for?"

He smoothed his hand over my hair again and met my eyes. "I came at you pretty hard just now. I didn't mean to go that hard. You just felt so good once I got inside you and those little sounds you make are so fucking hot, I just couldn't hold back. You seemed like you were with me, but..."

I smoothed a hand over his chest, trying to reassure him with my touch. "I was with you, Dante. Every single second I was with you. Did you notice I came so hard I almost blacked out? Twice? Believe me, I was with you."

Dante's body relaxed a little, but I could tell he wasn't completely convinced yet. "You'd tell me if I hurt you?"

I scooted up, laying across his chest to give him a kiss. "I would. I promise. You didn't. But I would tell you."

Seeming satisfied, Dante rolled us over so I was laying on my back with him next to me, arm bent, his head resting on his hand. He stroked his thumb across my cheek. He leaned in to give me a quick kiss then pulled back, moving his hand down to rest on my stomach.

"I missed you today."

"I missed you, too." I ran my hand up and down Dante's arm, loving the feel of his warm skin. "Was your day okay?"

"It started out weird. Pete showed up at the gym."

"What?" I stopped rubbing Dante's arm and looked up at him.

"Yeah, he was pissed about me telling Silas March on Saturday that I'm not going to fight again. He was spouting off about needing money, but I asked him why and he wouldn't say. Who knows. He stormed off, but he'll cool down. He had to know it wasn't going to happen. I've been telling him that for months."

"I guess he just didn't want to believe it."

"I guess not." Dante looked down at me, reaching up to play with a curl of hair that lay over my shoulder. "How about your day? Did you have fun with Meg tonight?"

"It was good. There was a strange guy at the hotel, but he didn't cause any problems, so it ended up being no big deal. And I had a great time catching up with Meg. She's dating some guy. I think I'm going to see if we can all go out together so we can meet him. Is that okay?"

Yawning, Dante rolled to his back, wrapping his arm around my waist and pulling me along with him.

"Whatever you want, baby."

Dante kissed the top of my head, then reached up to turn off the light.

~

I woke up the next morning when Dante kissed me goodbye. I rolled over, wishing I didn't have to spend the day away from Dante and wishing even more that I didn't have to go to work. As I'd told Dante, it wasn't my dream job. But until I figured out what was, I had bills to pay.

Groaning, I pushed myself out of bed. I was a little sore from my activities with Dante the past two nights, but I didn't regret any of it. I had some time before I headed to work, so I ate a semi-healthy breakfast, straightened my apartment, and did a load of laundry before getting ready to go.

The day at work was uneventful and thankfully the strange guy from the day before didn't reappear. At the end of my shift I walked out to the employee parking garage with Rachel and Troy who had worked the front desk that day. Troy happened to be parked right next to me on the rooftop of the garage and we commiserated over not being able to find better parking spots.

I knew that Dante had to work until at least 8pm, so I hit a drive thru for dinner. I pulled into the parking lot of my apartment building then headed to my apartment, hands full with my purse, work bag, carry-out bag and keys.

As I juggled everything to unlock my apartment door a chill suddenly ran down my spine. I spun around a second before I heard the scrape on the pavement behind me and came face to face with the strange guy from the hotel.

He stopped abruptly as he realized that I'd turned around to face him. He looked agitated and kept glancing at Dante's door like he expected Dante to step out and join us.

"You're Dante's girl, right? You're with him?"

His nonstop motion set me on edge almost as much as his words. My instincts were telling me not to give him too much information.

"Why are you asking me that? Who are you?" I kept my voice even, trying not to let him hear the panic I was starting to feel. I knew it was way too early for Dante to come home but I hoped for an early appearance anyway. This guy wasn't big, but he was wiry. And deliberately or not, he was blocking me from the stairs.

"I'm a friend of Dante's. And you're Mia. I know he's with you. I know it. Don't try to lie and say different."

I fought to stay calm. Was this Pete? What did he want with me? "Yes, you're right. I'm with Dante. I'd never lie about that. Are you Pete?"

"Yeah, yeah, I'm Pete."

Trying to stall for time while I figured out what to do, I said, "You were at the hotel I work at yesterday. Did you want to talk with me? Why were you there?"

My questions seemed to backfire. Pete scowled at me and spit on the floor at my feet. "Stupid bitch. I was waiting for you." He paced back and forth and muttered, almost like he was talking to himself. "Planned to grab you yesterday but you didn't fucking drive. Fucking friend picked you up. And today you were with that giant." He could only be referring to Troy, who was built like a linebacker. "Didn't want to grab you here. Gave me no choice."

As soon as he said the words "grab you" I felt behind me for my door. Could I get inside and get the door locked before he could get to me? I didn't know what was going through Pete's mind, but if he thought he was taking me somewhere without a fight he was wrong.

Suddenly Pete stopped pacing and pinned me with an intense stare. "I called him, you know. I did. He's on his way. He has to fight again. He'll do it in exchange for you. He will. He has to."

In exchange for me? What? With horror, I realized this guy might actually be crazy.

We heard footsteps pounding on the pavement below. Without warning, Pete lunged at me. I spun away, pushing at my door, scrambling frantically to get inside. The door slammed open, but just as I crossed the threshold, I felt Pete grab my hair. He yanked me back and the weight of my work bag and purse flying off my shoulder threw me off balance even more. I heard a crash inside my apartment, then Pete pulled me in front of him and gripped me hard around the waist, pinning my arms against me. I struggled, but Pete was stronger than he looked. Whether he was on something or it was just adrenaline giving him added strength, I couldn't break free.

Chapter 24

Dante

My heart stopped when I reached the top of the stairs. Pete had Mia, holding her in front of him like a shield. She was squirming in his hold, trying to fight back, but he had her arms trapped and she couldn't get any leverage. When she saw me, she stilled. I could see the fear in her eyes, but overlaying that was anger. She looked scared, but also pissed as hell.

"I'm sorry, Dante." Mia pushed back against Pete, but he held his ground.

"No, baby. Nothing for you to be sorry for." I kept my rage and terror clamped down, trying my best to reassure her.

Then I switched my gaze to Pete and let the rage show. I wanted him to see in my eyes how deeply he was going to regret ever touching Mia.

"Pete, hear me when I say this. If you so much as bruise her, I swear to God I will tear your arm off your body and beat you to death with it. Let her go now, and I'll give you the chance to run like hell."

Pete shook his head frantically. "Not until you say you'll fight." He tightened his hold on Mia and I heard her faint gasp. She wasn't meeting my eyes now. "If you agree to fight I'll let her go. I don't want to hurt her. You made me do this, Dante. You made me."

I took a step closer, looking for an angle to pull Pete away from

Mia. But he had her wrapped up too tightly. If I took him down, she would go with us and could get seriously hurt.

"I didn't make you do shit, Pete. I told you every time you brought it up that I wouldn't do it."

Suddenly Pete's face changed completely. Tears welled up in his eyes and he looked at me with desperation. "But you have to. I need the money, D. I have to have the money."

He'd said that before, but this time he sounded hopeless. "Why, Pete? Are you sick? Is your sister sick? Why do you need it?"

In the space of a second, Pete transformed again, from sad and desperate to raging and crazed, his eyes wild.

"To have a life! I need it so I can have a fucking life!"

He yanked Mia sideways and she gasped again, looking at me this time with pain in her eyes. Seeing that she was hurting made my heart twist. "My sister, ha!" Pete spit on the ground, yanking Mia back in the opposite direction. She closed her eyes and pulled on his arm, but couldn't seem to budge his hold. "The money is so I can get away from that bitch! So I can have a life without her riding my ass about getting a job, doing chores, all the fucking time! I deserve my own life!"

Out of patience, I stepped forward again. Pete jolted back, dragging Mia with him. That's when I saw the knife in his hand, pressed against Mia's stomach, and my lungs squeezed in my chest. I jerked my head up to meet Mia's eyes. She looked back at me, still scared but calm, seemingly ready for whatever I was going to do. I had to get that knife far away from her.

I looked back at Pete.

"For the last time, I'm not going to fight. It's not going to happen. I'm not worried about your life. But right now, you should be." I smiled at Pete without a trace of humor. I wanted him to feel every bit of my controlled rage and cold intent. "I'm going to give you one more chance, Pete. One final chance to save your own ass and get the hell out of here. Be smart, Pete. Take the chance I'm giving you. If I get my hands on you, I promise you I will beat you beyond recognition."

I was gambling that Pete would take the chance and run. My heart in my throat, I hoped I wasn't gambling with Mia's life. If Pete didn't turn her loose....

Pete's breathing picked up and his eyes darted between me and the stairs. I eased away from them a little, hoping to tempt him with what looked like a clear path. I knew that it wasn't, but there was no way he could know that even if he got away from me, Dev and Jamey were waiting below. But still he hesitated. I needed to push him more.

"Time's up, Pete. Turn her loose now and run."

Moving without warning, Pete spun and pushed Mia hard to the side as he scrambled in the opposite direction for the stairs. She cried out and as she fell, I saw blood on her arm and side. Without a thought for Pete, I ran for Mia as Pete flung himself frantically down the stairs, the knife falling and clattering to the ground. I heard a shout and thump and knew that Dev and Jamey had grabbed him. I reached Mia as she was sitting up, wincing.

Not knowing where she was injured and afraid to hurt her, I went to my knees next to her and cradled her cheek in my hand, turning her face up to mine. Seeing her blood was making me panic. I clamped down on it as hard as I could, but when I spoke my voice shook.

"Mia, baby, where are you hurt?"

"My arm." She winced again and I helped her lift her right arm. Bright red blood flowed from a long cut across the inside of her upper arm, likely made by the knife blade slicing through her as Pete pushed her away. Lowering her arm again gently, I swallowed hard. Knowing she was hurt and knowing it was my fault was almost too much to take. The need to go find Pete downstairs where I knew Dev and Jamey were holding him and to punch him again and again until my anger was gone was almost overwhelming. I knew I could kill him if I hit him full force, but in that moment I didn't even care. The only need stronger was the need to take care of Mia. I pulled her against me, cradling her against my chest. She leaned into me willingly and the tightness in my chest eased just a little.

"I'm sorry, baby. I should have gotten here sooner. Gotten him away from you somehow. I didn't see the knife at first. I didn't know…"

Imagining what could have happened, imagining Mia laying in my arms bleeding, I stuttered to a stop.

Mia leaned away a little and it was all I could do not to pull her back to me. I knew she was searching my face, but I couldn't look her in the eye. My mind swirled with the thought that I could have gotten her killed.

"Dante, look at me." As it always did, her soft voice slid into me, calming me and allowing me to breathe. I did as she asked. Looking into her pretty brown eyes, I knew with absolute certainty that I could not live without this woman.

"It's not your fault, Dante. You got here as fast as you could. And you heard him – he didn't mean to hurt me. I could feel that he had the knife, but I knew you couldn't tell. He was acting so crazy, I was afraid to say anything and maybe send him into a rage. I'll be okay, though. I promise."

I didn't say anything – couldn't – just pulled her close again, kissing the top of her head. She was wrong. No matter what she said, I was responsible and I knew it. But this was no time to argue with her.

Hearing sirens in the distance, I reluctantly let Mia go.

"Those are for us, I'm sure." I rose to my feet and helped Mia to hers.

She frowned at me as she stood. "But Pete's gone. Who would have...?"

"Pete's not gone. I'm sure Dev and Jamey grabbed him downstairs and called the police."

Mia walked toward the stairs with me, still clearly confused. She was limping just a little, but steady on her feet, which settled my heart a little more.

"Dev and Jamey are here? But how...?"

Stopping at the top of the stairs I turned to face her. "I promise I'll explain everything later, okay? Are you alright to go downstairs with me? The police will need to talk with you, but I know Pete's down there. I'd bring the police up here but I really I don't want to leave you up here by yourself."

Mia looked up at me, shaking her head. "No, I'm okay. I'll come downstairs."

Once we got downstairs, the next hour passed in a blur. The police secured Pete, combative as he was, leading him in handcuffs to a police car. Then each of us talked with an officer separately, recounting what had happened. The life squad arrived, called by the police when they'd seen the blood on Mia. They cleaned and bandaged the cut on her arm, which thankfully wasn't deep enough to need stitches, and cleaned the large scrapes on her other arm and leg where she'd slid along the ground when she fell.

As the police and life squad were preparing to leave, Mrs. Curr's door opened suddenly. She didn't step out, just stuck her head out and surveyed the whole scene critically. She zeroed in on Mia's bandaged arm, then looked directly at me. I braced myself to get blasted for disturbing her evening and was shocked when she inquired, "Everyone okay?"

I nodded and responded, still not sure she wasn't going to complain in some way. "Everyone's okay."

She simply nodded back briskly, replied, "Good, then. Keep it that way," and stepped back in her apartment.

Mia and I looked at each other and shrugged. Maybe Mrs. Curr wasn't just a cranky old busybody, after all. After all the shit she'd given me in the past, I'd reserve judgement for now.

We stood with Dev and Jamey as the police cars and life squad pulled away. Mia leaned against me, clearly exhausted. She looked at Dev and Jamey, her head tilted to the side a little.

"I still don't know how you guys ended up here with Dante but thank you. Thank you for being here and for grabbing Pete. Knowing he's not out there running around somewhere makes me feel a lot safer."

I'd already thanked the guys, but I knew it would mean a lot to them to hear it from Mia, as well. As for how they came to be there...

"The short version is that Dev was at the gym with me when Pete called saying he had you." What I didn't say was that Dev had pushed me out of the gym and into his Jeep, driving like a bat out of hell toward the apartment while I lost my shit. "And we called Jamey – Mia, this is Jamey; Jamey, Mia, by the way – for more backup on the way." Jamey had sprinted the blocks from the pub to the apartment, not wanting to take the time to get his car keys from his apartment above the pub. I was humbled and grateful that both he and Dev had literally dropped everything in a split second and run to help me and Mia. I owed them both, though they insisted I didn't.

"Well, this is a crazy way to meet you Jamey, but again, thank you both." Mia stepped forward, kissing first Dev then Jamey on the cheek before she stepped back next to me.

Jamey, in typical Jamey fashion, just shrugged and smiled. "Eh, right place, right time. Always glad to have a chance to help a friend and kick a little ass in the process."

"Well said and I couldn't agree more." Dev pulled out his keys. "I'm going to hit the road before the adrenaline crash hits me." Dev offered Jamey a ride and they headed toward the Jeep, still parked sideways almost on the sidewalk where we'd skidded to a stop earlier.

I turned to Mia, folding her into my arms and pulling her close. I felt her arms come around me as I kissed the top of her head, then rested my head against hers. I'd been touching her all night, had barely lost physical contact with her except when the police had talked with us separately to get our statements. I wanted to breathe her in, absorb her into me, and never be away from her again. I knew it was a reaction to seeing her in danger, seeing her scared and hurt. I'd have to be away from her at some point, but I was going to delay that as long as

I possibly could.

Stepping back, I looked down at my girl and she looked up at me. We stood that way, just looking at each other for a few seconds, then I leaned forward and kissed her on the nose, making her smile. Keeping my arm around her, we turned toward the steps and started upstairs.

Chapter 25

Mia

I stopped right outside my apartment door, noticing my forgotten carry-out dinner laying on the ground. I didn't even remember dropping it, but I obviously had. From the state of it, it looked like it had been stepped on at least once. Looking at it, I sighed.

"Well, so much for that."

Dante scooped it up.

"If you're brave enough to chance it, I can make us something. I need to eat, too."

"You know me, I'm a risk taker." Hearing Dante's quiet laugh made me feel worlds better. I knew he was blaming himself for everything that had happened. "Anything is fine with me."

I stepped into my apartment and stopped again.

My purse, work bag, and everything that had been on the table next to my door were scattered on the floor, the table laying on its side in the middle of the mess. My purse or work bag must have knocked the little table over when they'd swung off my shoulder as Pete grabbed me from behind. I looked mournfully at what was once my beautiful swirly pink lamp with the Christmas tinsel lampshade, now smashed to pieces.

"My lamp broke." I knew I was pouting but I couldn't help it.

"I see that, baby." Dante rubbed my back. "At least something good

163

came out of this whole thing."

His tone was so serious that it took me a minute to process what he'd said. Turning toward him, I could see the sparkle in his eyes. He wanted to smile, I could tell, but he was holding it in.

"Hey, that's mean." As Dante continued to fight his smile, I conceded defeat. "Okay, it's also kind of funny."

Dante's smile broke free and he hugged me. "I'm sorry, baby. I can't help it." He set me back on my feet and looked down at the pieces. "That thing was fuckin' ugly." Dante ran his hand over my hair. "I'll buy you a new one, okay?"

"It was beautiful, and you know it." Dante just shook his head solemnly, making me laugh. "Okay, fine, buy me a new one then."

"I'll buy you the best lamp ever." Dante kissed me on the top of my head and stepped away. "But right now, I'll figure out something for dinner. Do you need help changing first?"

I looked down at my ruined uniform. The top was streaked with blood from my cut and the skirt was torn from my fall. It was definitely going in the trash. What I really wanted was a shower, but I wasn't supposed to get my bandage wet. When I said that to Dante, he looked thoughtful for a second.

"How about this. Why don't you come over to my place and take a bath instead of a shower? It'll be easier to keep your bandage dry. I can fix us dinner while you're in the tub."

Dante's apartment was bigger than mine, with both a bathtub and a shower in the bathroom. His didn't have the tiny balcony that mine did, but I would have traded that in a second for a bathtub.

I agreed with Dante's plan and went to grab a change of clothes while he cleaned up the mess by my door. Before I knew it, I was soaking in Dante's tub, listening to the sounds of him moving around in the kitchen. It was all so homey, so…normal. It was hard to believe that mere hours before Pete was holding me with a knife against my stomach, pleading with Dante to fight again. Putting that firmly out of my mind, I tried to relax. I knew I'd replay the events in my head again and again, but for now, I was determined to set it aside and focus on being with Dante.

Dante made us grilled cheese and tomato soup – the perfect comfort food - for dinner. We ate it sitting at the tiny table in his kitchen. I'd intended to suggest that we watch a movie, but I could barely make it through dinner. It wasn't late, but I could hardly keep my head up. After my third huge yawn, I rested my elbow on the table and propped my head on my hand. I looked at Dante, my eyes getting sleepier by the second.

"I'm sorry, Dante. I think I need to turn in." The regret was clear in my voice and I was glad. I wanted Dante to hear how sad I was to leave him and go to my bed.

Dante reached across the table and covered my hand with his. "Don't apologize, Mia. It's been a crazy night." Dante squeezed my hand a bit. He met my eyes, a question in his. "Can I ask one thing, though?" At my nod, Dante went on. "Will you stay here with me tonight? I want to be close to you, to know you're safe. We don't have to do anything, I promise. That's not what this is about." The look in Dante's eyes was intense. He was looking at me like...like I was his whole world. Out of nowhere, the thought appeared in my mind that he was fast becoming my whole world, too. The thought didn't surprise me, didn't scare me. It just felt right. I stood up and crossed to Dante, stepping between his legs and wrapping my arms around his neck and shoulders. I felt his arms wrap around my hips, holding me close. I dipped my head close to his ear.

"Of course, I'll stay. I need to be close to you, too."

Dante squeezed me tight for a second, then without warning, leaned forward a little and stood up with me draped over his shoulder. I shrieked a little and felt his body shake as he chuckled. When we reached the bedroom, he set me down gently on my feet then patted me on my butt. Both of us sobered a minute when I pulled off the t-shirt I'd changed into and Dante saw the shallow cuts that Pete's knife had left on my stomach. I'd felt the knife cutting me through my shirt as Pete had gotten more agitated and had held me tighter, but with everything else that had happened I'd forgotten about them. Wishing I'd waited until Dante was in the shower before getting undressed, that I'd been more careful about him seeing the cuts, all I could do was run my hands up and down his arms, trying to soothe him as he ran his fingers across my stomach, just barely touching my skin. I saw him swallow hard, then he looked up at me, his eyes full of rage and pain.

"I should have killed him." His voice was so low, it was almost a whisper. "I should have killed him when I had the chance."

Knowing he wouldn't listen to reason right then, I stepped forward, wrapped my arms around him and held him tight. His arms came around me and I felt him bury his face in my hair.

"I'm okay, Dante. I'm right here. I'm okay."

I repeated the same thing over and over again, slipping my hands under his shirt and smoothing them over the warm skin of his back until I felt him relax again. Finally, he pulled back, captured my mouth in a long, slow kiss, then patted me on the butt again as he headed for the shower.

By the time he slipped into bed behind me, I was almost asleep. He curved his body around mine, his arm wrapped carefully across my stomach. I felt him kiss my ear, then whisper, "Night, baby" as I drifted off, safe and warm, next to the man I was falling in love with.

⌒

The next few weeks passed quietly, drama-free except for a couple of court appearances to testify in front of the grand jury for Pete's case and to attend his sentencing. He'd pled guilty to all charges, so at least we were spared going through a trial. Pete had been held in the county jail since his arrest, unable to post bail, and he was pale and subdued in court. A woman who had to be his sister sat in the back corner of the courtroom, slipping out at the end of the proceedings before we could speak with her. I found out much later that Dante had gone to her house to check on her and make sure Pete's arrest hadn't caused her any problems. As it turned out, it had made her life easier. While she wasn't glad that he'd gotten himself into trouble, a lot of stress was gone from her life with his absence.

Dante and I spent every free moment with each other, including sleeping in the same bed each night, either in his apartment or in mine. Most nights we made sweet, slow love or had fast, hard sex, depending on our mood. Other nights, Dante just wrapped himself around me and held me while we slept. I still had a few rough nights filled with dreams of Pete grabbing me and I knew Dante did, as well. He did his very best to keep his protective instincts under control, giving me as much space as he could stand while still keeping an eye on me. I understood how scared he was at the thought that he could have lost me. I knew that I was in love with Dante and I thought that he felt the same for me, but I hadn't had the courage yet to say the words. It seemed like I should wait, like it was still too soon. When I said it, I wanted Dante to have no doubt that I meant it. We spent a lot of time at the pub and I got to know Dante even better through his friends' eyes. It was clear that when they said they were all brothers they felt that down to their souls. They opened their arms to me without question, embracing me both literally and figuratively because I was with Dante.

The one flaw during those perfect weeks was that I rarely saw Meg.

It was partly because I was spending every waking moment with Dante, true, but also because Meg was splitting her time between traveling for work and spending time with her new man, Aaron. All I'd heard for weeks was, "Aaron says..." and "Aaron thinks..." and I was anxious to meet the guy. Meg and I texted, talked, or chatted via FaceTime almost every day, but we hadn't had a chance for the 4 of us to get together.

Finally, we nailed down a date to meet Meg and Aaron at the pub. I was just getting ready to step in the shower that evening when I heard the door to my apartment open and close. Dante and I each had a key to each other's apartment and went back and forth between apartments constantly.

"I'm in here, Dante."

I heard Dante's footsteps in the hall then he appeared in the doorway to the bathroom.

"Hey, ba...oh hell yeah." Dante scanned my naked body head to toe, his eyes growing dark, the fire inside heating instantly. He reached out a hand and stroked one of my nipples, which puckered and grew hard under his touch.

His eyes still on my body, he drew in a breath. "You are so beautiful, Mia."

No one had ever made me feel as wanted and loved as Dante. Everything in me wanted to lean into his touch, but I knew we'd be late if I gave in. So I stepped back, swatting at Dante's hand.

"I can't, Dante. I barely have enough time for a shower."

Eyes on my face now, Dante stepped closer. Hands resting on my hips, he leaned in, nuzzling his cheek against mine, then kissing his way down my neck to my collarbone, and back up to my neck again.

"I can't help it, baby. I see you and I want you. I think about you and I want you." Dante ran his hands up my sides, pulling me closer.

I knew I should protest, but instead I lifted my chin, giving him better access as he continued to nibble on my neck. I pulled him closer, needing to feel him pressed against me. It was always like this. Dante touched me and I was lost.

Dante lifted me, setting me down on the sink counter and stepping between my legs. My eyes on his, I reached for the button of his jeans, releasing it, then slowly lowering his zipper. He hissed as my fingers brushed against his hard dick, his head back and his eyes squeezed closed. Pushing his jeans and briefs out of the way, I wrapped my hand around him, stroking him from base to tip. Lowering his head, Dante placed his hand over mine and lined himself up with my entrance. He pushed inside me and groaned.

"You feel so good. So tight and warm."

He withdrew a little, then slid back in, filling me and setting me on fire. I wrapped my legs around his waist, holding on as Dante set the perfect pace. In minutes, I hit my peak, shaking and clinging to Dante as I came. As I started to come down, Dante's breathing grew rougher just seconds before he pulled out of me and came on my stomach with a groan. Still shaking, he dropped his forehead on mine. We stayed that way, just breathing together for a minute, then Dante kissed me and stepped away.

"I'll let you take your shower. I'll be back in a bit."

Tucking himself back in his jeans, Dante stepped out of the bathroom. Still in a bit of a daze I looked over at the clock on the bathroom wall and jumped. Darn Dante! His sexy ass had barely left me enough time. Jumping in the shower, I rushed to get ready for the evening ahead.

~

We were running late by the time we got to the pub. Thanks to Dante's interruption I'd had to get ready in record time. My hair was still damp from the quick shower I'd had to take, but I'd managed to pull together a decent outfit. This was my first time meeting Aaron and I was nervous. I couldn't get a good read from Meg on how much she really liked this guy and that was unusual. I could usually tell just from how she talked about a guy, but Aaron seemed different. I was anxious to meet him and see how they were together. This was also the first time that Dante and Meg were going to spend time together. I knew that would go fine, but I was looking forward to having two of the most important people in my life together.

As soon as we walked into the pub, I spotted Meg sitting at the bar with a man sitting next to her. I started that way with Dante following me. Kendrick, busy behind the bar as always, saw us and lifted a hand in greeting. Meg saw us too, waved, and leaned over to say something to Aaron. They were both standing up from their stools when we reached them. Meg met me with a quick hug.

"Hey, you made it. I was getting worried."

Ever since Pete had grabbed me, Meg had been like a mother hen. Even though I'd never been in any real danger, the incident had spooked Meg almost as badly as it had Dante. Meg could seem a little cool to people who didn't know her, but once you were in her circle, she loved you with everything she had."

"I know. I'm sorry. It's Dante's fault."

I didn't look at Dante as I said it, but I knew he'd have a smirk on his face. Before he could say anything that would embarrass me, I turned to the man standing next to Meg.

"Hi, you must be Aaron."

I got that much out and extended my hand for him to shake, but my brain stopped there. I knew I was staring but I couldn't help it. This guy was 100% absolutely, stunningly gorgeous. His features were male perfection – square jaw, high cheekbones, straight nose, and lips that looked like they were meant to kiss. The combination of his black hair, sapphire blue eyes, and beautiful smile was devastating. He was about 6 feet tall, just a few inches taller than me, but not quite as tall as Dante.

I realized he was talking, and I felt Dante's chest bump against my back as I saw his hand reach past me to shake Aaron's. Feeling Dante press against my back as he leaned forward helped snap me out of my daze and focus on what Aaron was saying.

"…been looking forward to meeting both of you. I'm glad the timing worked out tonight."

"Me, too." I was glad I got that out and it sounded pretty normal. Meg was giving me the eye like she knew Aaron's model good looks had knocked me off balance for a minute. It seemed like she was enjoying my surprise.

"Do you two want to get some drinks and then we can grab a table?"

Before either Dante or I could respond to Meg's question, Jamey stepped out of the back. He was headed behind the bar, but when he saw us he detoured around the front. He did that male handshake - half hug thing that guys do with Dante, then turned to give me a one-armed hug and kiss on the cheek. I'd learned early on that Jamey was physically very affectionate, so a hug or a kiss on the cheek from him didn't faze me.

I greeted Jamey, then turned to introduce him to Meg and Aaron.

"Jamey, this is my best friend Meg and her friend, Aaron."

They all shook hands as I continued on. "And this is Jamey. He's one of Dante's best friends and the chef here."

Jamey turned to smile at me but shook his head.

"I'm just the main cook and I run the kitchen. I appreciate the compliment, honey, but let's not exaggerate things by calling me a chef."

Dante reached out and squeezed Jamey's shoulder.

"Jamey's way too humble. Well, about his food, anyway. He may be 'just the cook' but his food is amazing."

"Yeah, I do okay." Jamey's grin was just this side of cocky. His response made him sound like he was talking about something other than food.

"You guys hungry?" Jamey asked, looking at the 4 of us.

I was starving, but even if I hadn't been there was no way I was turning down food from Jamey.

Dante and I confirmed that we were, then turned to Meg and Aaron. Meg looked to Aaron for a response, surprising me a bit. Meg was usually pretty outspoken, but she was deferring to Aaron to say if she was hungry?

"Sure. We could eat something." Aaron confirmed with a glance over at Meg.

"Just whatever you feel like, Jamey." Dante said, then looked over at Meg and Aaron again to confirm that was okay. We never ordered off the pub's menu, just let Jamey make something for us. He often used us to test out possible new menu items and we'd never had anything we didn't like. "Unless you guys have something you want or things you hate or something?"

Aaron confirmed he'd try anything. Meg agreed but added, "But maybe something...not fried and greasy or swimming in processed cheese? Something a little healthier, if that's possible?"

Meg's voice held a note of doubt like she questioned whether Jamey could come up with anything that fit that description. It was a little bit of an insult to Jamey, but I was sure it was unintentional. Meg was obsessed with what she ate, and she usually studied restaurant menus before she ordered like she'd be tested on them later.

Jamey's smirk told me that he'd picked up on the insult, intentional or not, and that he was taking it as a challenge. I cringed a little – Jamey and Meg weren't exactly making a great first impression on each other.

"Sure. I think I can manage that." Jamey's dry tone made Meg frown a little like she was puzzled at his response. Before she could say anything, Jamey clapped Dante on the back and headed to his original destination behind the bar.

By that time, Kendrick had placed our usual drinks up on the bar for us, so we grabbed them, waved our thanks to him as he served another customer, and headed to a table.

As we walked to the table, Meg spoke up.

"What was that? Was it wrong to ask for some healthy food? What the hell?"

She was clearly confused and offended by Jamey's response.

"No, not at all." I tried to smooth her ruffled feathers. "It was just... the way you said it you made it sound like you doubted Jamey was capable of anything more than greasy burgers and nachos."

"No, I didn't!" Meg protested my comment. We reached a table and I was glad to see Aaron pull out a stool for Meg. As she scooted up to the table, she looked at me in question. I just looked back at her. "Wait, did I?"

Aaron answered for me. "You kind of did, babe."

Dante nodded and agreed. "Yeah, a little. But don't worry, Meg. Jamey has thick skin. It'll roll right off him. Just be prepared to be surprised by whatever he comes up with."

"Well, crap, Dante." Meg looked defeated. "The first time I meet one of your best friends – who happens to run the kitchen at your other best friends' pub – and the first thing I do is insult him."

"It's okay, Meg." I reached over and squeezed her hand. "He won't take it that seriously." At least I hoped he wouldn't. If Dante and I worked out long term – and I definitely hoped we did – Meg and Jamey would inevitably be spending time around each other. Hopefully, this bumpy start wouldn't be a problem later.

Thankfully, Aaron changed the subject, mentioning that the pub reminded him of one he'd visited on his frequent trips to the UK for work. That got us talking about travel, with Aaron the clear winner in the number of countries he'd visited. It struck me as a bit odd that he essentially turned the conversation into a competition, but I reminded myself that he might be nervous, too, and just trying to impress us with his world travels.

Before I could give it much more thought, a server brought our food to our table. The fact that Jamey didn't bring it himself had me glancing at Dante with concern. Jamey always brought our food out to us and often told us something about it and stayed while we tried it. What if Jamey had taken Meg's inadvertent insult to heart and was avoiding her? He wasn't usually touchy, but... Dante looked back at me and shrugged. Maybe I was borrowing trouble reading so much into this. It was a busy night and the kitchen might be crazy. And we weren't sitting at the bar like we normally did, making it less convenient for Jamey to bring us the food himself. Determined to put it out of my mind, I dug into the food along with the others.

Jamey had sent us house-made hummus with warm pita triangles and fresh veggies, two kinds of sliders – beef and portabella mushroom – three different flatbreads, and a huge basket of baked sweet potato fries, which Jamey knew were my favorite.

As always, the food was delicious. Jamey used local suppliers whenever he could and used the freshest ingredients he could get his hands on. The difference really showed. After several minutes of stuffing our faces, Meg sighed loudly.

"Okay, I admit it. Jamey is a god. This is some of the best food I've had in a long time. This hummus is amazing and I'm seriously having to resist stabbing you all with my fork so I can keep the portabella sliders to myself."

We all laughed as Dante quickly pulled his hand away from the last portabella slider. Smiling at Meg, he slid the serving plate her way.

"All yours, Meg. I never argue with a woman armed with a fork."

Meg reached for the slider, smiling back at Dante as she set it on the small plate in front of her.

"I'm not even going to try to act polite and let you have it."

Aaron leaned into Meg a bit, knife in hand. "Spilt it with me, babe?"

He reached over and cut the slider in two, not even checking for a response from Meg. Meg's eyes flashed with irritation for a second, then she smiled at Aaron.

"Of course I will. I probably shouldn't eat the whole thing anyway."

Aaron winked at Meg. "Good point. I'll help you out."

Maybe it was the fact that Dante had just been a gentleman and given the slider to Meg so willingly, but Aaron seemed like kind of a jerk to me in that moment. It wasn't a big deal really and Meg had said it was okay – well, after Aaron had clearly already assumed it was – but still. There was plenty of other food left. What did it hurt to let Meg have her favorite thing? And that comment about eating the whole thing? What was that? It was a small slider with veggies on it – how bad could it be to eat the whole thing? Meg usually ate healthy, but she ate. Curious as to what was going on, I tried to catch her eye, but she kept looking over by the bar where the door to the kitchen was. A minute or two later, Meg hopped down from her stool abruptly.

"I'll be right back."

Jamey had come out of the kitchen and was standing behind the bar talking to Kendrick about something. As Meg hurried in his direction, he turned to go back in the kitchen, then stopped and turned back toward Meg like she'd called his name. He stood and listened to whatever Meg was saying to him, then shrugged. I couldn't read Jamey's expression, but at least he didn't seem angry or annoyed. Meg extended her hand. After a few seconds, Jamey took her hand, said something, then turned and disappeared through the kitchen door. Meg stood there looking at the kitchen door, then shook her head and started back to the table.

I turned back to Dante and Aaron. While I'd been watching Meg and Jamey, Dante and Aaron had finished off the flatbreads and launched into a conversation about some expensive truck Aaron was thinking about buying. As they talked, Dante caught my eye and raised his eyebrows. I realized that he'd caught the encounter between Meg and Jamey and, like me, was curious about what had been said. Aaron, on the other hand, seemed like he either hadn't noticed or he didn't care.

Meg reached the table and climbed back up on her stool. I could tell from her expression that the conversation had gone fine – Meg was not one to hide it when she was pissed off – but I asked anyway.

"Everything ok?"

Meg smiled - her normal, natural smile - and my remaining concern melted away.

"Sure. I apologized, Jamey graciously accepted, and we're all good."

I was sure there was more to it than that, but as long as everything was settled, I supposed it wasn't really any of my business. The conversation turned back to the truck Aaron was considering buying, which made Meg groan and roll her eyes.

"Aaron, the car you have is beautiful. It's not even two years old!"

"I know, babe." Aaron looked over at Meg. "But the truck is better. Only the best, right?"

"I know." Meg conceded. "But it seems like sometimes great should be enough, you know?"

Aaron frowned and shook his head. "You know I don't agree with that. You should always strive to have the best, to be the best." He looked over at Dante. "You agree with that, Dante, right? You were a champion fighter. You don't get anywhere being second best."

Dante was leaned back in his seat, his big hand resting on my thigh. He looked relaxed and happy and I loved seeing him like this. He looked over at me with a smile and squeezed my leg lightly.

"Well, when it comes to Mia, I agree. Nothing but the best." I wrinkled my nose at him, making him laugh.

He looked back to Aaron and picked up his drink with his free hand. "Other than that, yeah, I think you should work to be your best. Whatever *your* best is. Doesn't always mean you'll come out on top, but if it's important to you, give it your all and let the chips fall. I think the trick is deciding what's most important to you. Like Meg said, I think sometimes great is enough. I don't necessarily consider something 'second best' if it gives me what I need."

Aaron pointed at Dante. "That's where we disagree, my friend." He leaned forward on the table, radiating intensity. This was obviously something he felt strongly about. "Take Meg, for example." He looked over at Meg and she tilted her head at him, like she wasn't sure what he was going to say next. "She's the youngest senior consultant her company has ever had. Her past clients bring her back again and again. She's seen as an expert in half a dozen areas. She could be happy with that. Hell, she could coast the rest of her career on that. But instead, she's going to get her MBA." I looked at Meg in surprise. I hadn't heard anything about this from her. "Once she gets that, I guarantee she'll be a director within two years and a VP within five. If she plays her cards right, she'll be running that whole place within ten."

"I don't know about that." Meg glanced over at Aaron, then back at me. "Aaron suggested I look into getting my MBA online. I can get promoted without it, but having some kind of advanced degree will definitely be an advantage. And you know how my parents have always pushed education. They'd be thrilled. It seems like a win-win."

Meg was saying all of the right things, but underneath her words it felt like she was trying to convince me. Or maybe trying to convince herself?

"I think that's great, Meg. If that's something you want, I think you should go for it."

Meg looked relieved, like she had expected me to push back. She glanced over at Aaron again. "It's going to be crazy trying to fit it in with all of the traveling for work, but I really think it's something I should pursue."

Aaron smiled at Meg, his approval clear. "Absolutely, babe. It's one hundred percent something you should do. I'll be so proud of you when you can list those letters behind your name."

I reached across the table and patted Meg's arm. "I'm proud of you right now for going after something you want."

"I agree. A toast to Meg." Dante sat forward and lifted his glass, waiting while the rest of us did the same. "For getting in there, kicking ass, and taking names. May all your dreams come true."

"Aw thanks, Dante." Meg clinked her glass against his.

"And may your eyes not cross and fall out from the many, many hours you're about to spend online."

We all laughed and clinked glasses again. We talked for a few more minutes, then Aaron announced that it was time for Meg and him to call it a night. Dante and I decided to stay and try to catch Kendrick for a few minutes. While the guys shook hands, Meg gave me a quick hug and promised to call me, then she and Aaron headed for the door and we headed for the bar.

Dante's favorite seat at the far end of the bar was open, so we headed that way. Kendrick saw us coming and met us as we took our seats. He got us each an ice water at our request and slid them on to the bar in front of us.

"So, how'd things go?" Kendrick leaned his hip against the counter behind the bar and crossed his arms over his chest, the position showing off his toned arms and shoulders. Kendrick wasn't as built as Dante. His body didn't immediately grab your attention the way Dante's did. But if you took a minute to look, it was obvious he was in really good shape. With brown hair and smokey gray eyes, he was a good-looking guy.

"Okay, I guess." Even I could hear the lack of excitement in my voice.

"That good, huh?" Kendrick glanced over at a group sitting farther down the bar that had started talking loudly and stepped closer, resting his hands on the top of the bar. "I saw that your friend had something to say to Jamey, but it looked friendly enough."

"Yeah, that part was fine. It was just…"

I hesitated and Kendrick nodded.

"Ah, so you didn't like her guy."

I slumped back in my seat. "Ugh, is it that obvious?" I looked over at Dante. "Do you think Meg thinks I don't like him?'

Dante took a sip of his water. "Um…if I follow that, no I don't think Meg thinks that. I think you were perfectly friendly. You've been friends with Meg forever. She would have given you the eye or something if she thought you were acting weird toward Aaron."

Kendrick agreed. "I'm sure you were perfectly fine, Mia. You're about the friendliest person I know."

I hoped they were right.

"It's not that I didn't like Aaron. I mean, not exactly. He just seems kind of…high pressure, maybe? Like he's the one who has to make the decisions. Like he has super high expectations and Meg had better live up to them. Meg's been pushed by her parents her whole life. She doesn't need a man who does that crap, too. Like that whole thing about 'I'll be so proud of you when you have MBA behind your name.' He should be proud of her now!"

I could feel my irritation rising, annoyed on behalf of my best friend.

"He'd just listed all of these great things about her – youngest senior consultant, her expertise, blah, blah, blah – why isn't he proud of all that? Why does she need an MBA to make him proud? Shouldn't the person you're with be proud of you, proud to be with you, just because of the person you are? I mean, accomplishments are great and all and of course you want to celebrate them, but that's not what being with someone is about."

Kendrick and Dante just looked at me as I went on. I knew I was ranting a bit, but I was on a roll.

"Like me and Dante. He won a title and of course that's amazing and I'm happy he was able to do that. But I'd be with Dante if he'd never won a match in his life. And I'd be just as proud of him because of the man he is. That's the way it should be, right? It shouldn't be like, achieve this and then I'll be proud of you. It shouldn't work that way."

I picked up my water and took a sip. Kendrick and Dante looked at each other, then back at me.

"She's fierce when she's wound up, isn't she?" Kendrick said looking at me.

Dante huffed out a laugh and reached over to hold my hand. "Yeah, it's always the quiet ones, right?"

"Hello, sitting right here. I can hear you." Dante and Kendrick laughed.

"Fine." I pouted a little, but I knew they weren't really making fun of me. "I'm right, though."

Dante leaned over and kissed me on the cheek. "Yes, you're right, baby. That's exactly how it should be."

"I agree. That's how it should work." As he talked, Kendrick scanned the bar, making sure everyone was taken care of, then shifted his focus back to me. "But your friend seems to like him, so…"

"I just really don't know what she sees in him. She has guys asking her out all the time, so what's so special about him? I mean, he's obviously gorgeous."

That earned me a poke in the ribs and a look from Dante.

"Oh, come on. You'd have to be blind not to see how hot he is." Hearing nearly identical grunts from both Dante and Kendrick, but no other acknowledgement of what I'd said, I rolled my eyes at them and went on.

"But he doesn't seem right for Meg, you know?"

"I agree with you, but that's Meg's call, right?" Dante reached out and tugged lightly on a piece of my hair. "You don't like people telling you what to do, right?"

I grumbled but had to concede that Dante had a point. "I don't and yes, it's Meg's call but still. I won't give her my opinion unless she asks but if she does, I'm not going to lie to her."

"Sounds like a good compromise." Kendrick waved casually to two women who called their good-byes to him as they stepped away from the bar. They both looked disappointed that their departure hadn't garnered more attention from him. Maybe it was mean of me, but their glum expressions made me smile. Kendrick got hit on constantly. Like all day, every day, by loads of women. Even a guy or two occasionally, though he didn't swing that way. He always reacted in the same way, which is to say, not at all. He was always friendly in his own lowkey way, but he never rose to any of the bait that was dangled in front of him. I was sure he noticed it – he wasn't dumb or oblivious – but for whatever reason, he just chose not to acknowledge it. You would think after a while the ladies would quit trying, but they clearly didn't consider that an option.

One of the bartenders waved Kendrick over, needing him to take care of some transaction. Dante and I were ready to head out, so we said our goodbyes. We'd driven rather than walking from the apartment since we were already running late. When we got to the truck, Dante helped me up into the seat, then shut my door and walked around to the driver's side as I fastened my seatbelt. Since I was wearing jeans, I didn't really need his help, but he always helped me anyway. Same with getting out of the truck when we got home. I liked his hands on me and he liked putting them there, so who was I to argue?

As we walked up the stairs to our apartments, Dante asked me the question that had become our norm every evening.

"Yours or mine?"

We spent every night together. The only question was which apartment we stayed in. We each kept clothes and basic toiletries in both apartments, so it was convenient to stay in either.

"Yours," I decided. "Your bed is bigger. You hog too much of mine." Dante had a king-size bed, I had a queen. It almost seemed too big when I was in it alone, but with Dante's big frame in it, it rapidly became too small. "I practically had to sleep on top of you last night."

Dante nuzzled my neck from behind as he steered us toward his door and I tipped my head to the side to give him better access.

"I told you before, any time you want to be on top, you just let me know." His voice was husky and I could feel him getting hard as he pressed against me from behind.

"You'd like that, huh?" It was a rhetorical question, really, since I knew he would. I hadn't been confident enough to be on top yet, but I was still fired up from my defense of Meg earlier, so maybe tonight was the night.

"You know I'd love it." One arm firmly around my waist, Dante reached around me to unlock the door and push it open.

"Alright then." We stepped inside and I moved away from Dante. "Last one to the bedroom is on the bottom!"

I took off in the direction of the bedroom while Dante stood completely still by the front door. "Go, baby, go," he called as I turned, laughing, and backed toward the bedroom.

"Aren't you coming?" I stood just outside the bedroom door, tilting my head in invitation as I let my eyes run over him.

Dante's dark eyes blazed and I could see the tension in his body from across the apartment.

"I will be. And you will be, too. Again and again. Just as soon as you step inside that bedroom."

Holding his gaze, I slowly stepped backwards into the bedroom, beckoning him with one finger. As soon as I crossed the threshold of the room, Dante moved, vaulting over the back of the couch and reaching me with lightning speed. I shrieked as he tackled me, rolling us as we hit the bed so I was on top.

"You win, baby." Dante grinned up at me as I straddled him, his hands on my hips, eyes burning into mine. "You can ride me all night long if you want. Go ahead and have your way with me."

I leaned down to kiss him, rubbing slowly against the hard bulge nestled between my legs. Hearing Dante groan, knowing how much he wanted me, made me bolder.

"Why, thank you, cowboy. I think I just might."

And I did.

Chapter 26

Dante

I woke up early in my favorite position, with Mia draped across me. She'd been bolder in bed last night than she'd ever been, riding me, taking what she needed. She was always beautiful, but seeing her face above me as she came, she was stunning. If I hadn't already been head over heels in love with her, I would fallen hard right then. After what she'd said about me at the pub, how she was proud to be with me just because of the man I was, I wouldn't have stood a chance. I'd had to fight hard not to let the emotion show, not to tell her right then and there that I loved her.

I'd decided in that moment to bite the bullet and ask her to move in with me. We were living in both spaces, spending every night together, anyway. I just wanted to make it official and move her in with me. And I wanted to tell her I loved her, too. I'd thought it in my head so many times. I wanted to say it out loud, needed Mia to hear me say it. I knew it was too soon. We hadn't been together that long. If she couldn't say it back yet, that was okay. I had no doubt she felt it, but if she couldn't say the words yet, I'd wait until she was ready. If I had to wait forever for Mia, I would do it.

I had a plan in mind, a way to ask her, and it started with break-fast in bed. I slipped out of bed slowly and paused as Mia rolled over and snuggled back into the pillows. A short time later, I was walking back into the bedroom, Mia's favorite breakfast – scrambled eggs with cheese and mushrooms and coffee with vanilla creamer – in my hands. She was sitting up in bed stretching, so it was perfect timing. I took that as a good sign.

"Morning, baby. I made breakfast."

"Wow, thanks." Mia smiled as I set the plate and coffee cup on the bedside table. "Could you hand me something to put on?"

"It's a shame to cover all that beauty, but since you asked nicely..." I pulled a pair of Mia's panties and one of my t-shirts out of a drawer and tossed them to her. I could have grabbed her one of her own t-shirts, but I liked seeing her in mine. I guess I had some caveman left in me after all.

I sat next to her on the bed and we talked about unimportant stuff as she ate. As she was finishing up, I stood up and walked over to the closet, pulling a wrapped box down from the highest shelf. I carried it over to the bed and sat on the side closest to Mia, facing her. I felt my nerves start to rise. The next few minutes could be some of the most important ones of my life. I was sure of Mia, sure of how she felt about me, but that didn't stop the knots from forming in my stomach. Pushing the nerves down, I handed the box to Mia.

"I got you a present." Good, my voice sounded normal, even.

Mia's eyes lit up as she took the box from me.

"Breakfast in bed and a present? Did I forget it's my birthday?" Mia laughed and I couldn't help but smile. The knots in my stomach loosened just a bit.

"Nope, no birthday. Just something I promised you."

"Hm, something you promised me." Mia turned the box this way and that, like she was trying to guess what it was, then set it down on the bed, pulling off the paper. The box was plain brown, so she still wasn't able to tell what it was. She finally got the top pulled open and looked inside.

"A lamp!" She looked up at me, eyes shining, looking as excited as a kid at Christmas. "You bought me a lamp!" She leaned forward and kissed me quickly, then sat back and reached in the box to pull out the lamp. I held the box for her as she pulled the lamp free and held it up to admire it.

The lamp had a shiny silver base, skinny at the top then sloping down into a fat, rounded bottom. But I'd really bought it for her because of the lamp shade. The lamp shade was covered with strands of multi-colored beads that swung as Mia moved the lamp around. The shade was translucent, so according to the description, the light would shine through the shade and reflect off the beads when the light was turned on. It wasn't anywhere near as ugly as Mia's lamp that had gotten smashed to pieces, but it was quirky enough that I thought she might like it. Judging from the expression on her face, I'd been right.

"Dante, it's perfect. I absolutely love it. Thank you." She leaned in to give me another kiss.

"Good, I'm glad you like it."

This was the moment I'd planned for, time to ask her to move in with me. I took a breath and jumped.

"You can keep it on one condition."

Mia looked at me, puzzled. "Okay, what's that?"

"I want you to keep it here, along with the rest of your things. All of your things."

Mia frowned a little, still confused. "You want...my things?

Taking the lamp from her and setting it aside, I held her hands in mine and looked into her eyes.

"I want you to move in with me, Mia. I want us to live together, to be together. Or if you like your apartment better, I'll move in with you. I don't care where we are. I just want to be with you."

Mia was gripping my hands tight, her eyes locked on mine, not making a sound. I wasn't sure she was even breathing. I decided to lay all my cards on the table, to say the words I'd wanted to say for weeks.

"I'm in love with you, Mia. I love you. It might be too soon, I don't know. I just know how I feel. I love you and I want to live with you. Say you'll move in with me, Mia."

Tears welled up in Mia's eyes. I had a second to panic, then she let go of my hands and jumped into my lap, hugging me tight.

"Yes, Dante. Yes, I'll move in with you." Her words were muffled where her mouth was pressed against my neck, but I'd heard the yes that I needed. Then she pulled back and gave me even more. Tears running down her face, she put her hands on my cheeks and said the best words I'd ever heard.

"I love you, too, Dante. I do. I don't care if it's too soon. It's plenty of time to know I love you. That's all that matters."

Tipping her backward, I laid her on the bed, leaned over her and kissed her.

"You're all that matters. You're my whole world."

"And you're mine." Mia ran her hands down my arms, her touch both soothing me and setting me on fire as always.

"I meant it when I said that I don't care where we live. If you like your apartment better, we'll live there."

Mia was shaking her head even as I was talking.

"No, your apartment is bigger and you have a tub. Besides, that amazing couch of yours would never fit in my apartment. I'm not giving up that couch."

I grinned down at her. "Who knew all I had to do was let you sit on my couch and I had you?"

Mia grinned back, then sighed. "The perfect couch, the perfect lamp, and the perfect man. What else could I ever want?"

I leaned in, kissing her soft and slow. "Whatever you want, whatever you need, you'll have it, baby. You've given me everything, Mia, everything I could ever hope for and more. I promise you, with everything I am, I'm going to give you everything you could hope for right back."

Chapter 27

Mia

I stood looking around the kitchen of my apartment, checking to make sure everything was ready. People were due to start arriving at any minute and I still felt like I had a dozen things to do. Dante and I were hosting a party to celebrate the great news that he and Dev had gotten that week. The Webers, who Dante and I had talked with at the sponsor event a few weeks before, and a local corporate sponsor had decided to help fund the expansion of the youth program. With the funding from both, Dev and Dante were going to be able to make all the renovations they had planned and add another trainer.

I heard my apartment door open and Dante stepped into the kitchen. I'd agreed to move in with Dante the week before, but for the moment we were still living in both places. I was negotiating with the landlord about my lease and we were hoping to get him to agree to let Jamey take it over. Jamey's space above the pub was convenient for work, but it was a small studio. My apartment wasn't huge by any means, but it would give him more space and still be just a few blocks from the pub.

Dante crossed to me and gave me a quick kiss.

"Hey, baby, Jamey's here. Where do you want the food?"

"In here is good. Just anywhere on the counter or breakfast bar works for now."

Dante headed out to help Jamey while I moved the coolers that were sitting in the way. Soon they'd be filled with ice and drinks from the fridge in Dante's place. We were using the big open-air landing between my apartment and Dante's as a sort of patio for our party. It was plenty big for the group we had coming and we weren't blocking anyone's way to their apartment since we were on the top floor. We didn't have any set schedule for the party, so with the food set up in my kitchen and drinks in coolers outside, I figured that people could grab things as they wanted them. Jamey, bless him, was bringing a bunch of food from the pub. I'd made a mountain of chocolate chip cookies and brownies for dessert and left it at that.

I opened my apartment door just in time to see Jamey and Dante coming up the last of the stairs, each carrying several large pans.

"Honey, I'm home," Jamey joked as he walked toward me.

"Hopefully you'll be able to say that for real when you walk through this door sometime soon." I stepped back and held the door as first Jamey then Dante walked past me into the kitchen.

"Yeah, that'll be good. I'm ready to have a little more room to stretch out." Jamey set the stack of pans he was carrying down on the breakfast bar. "I hear the next door neighbors can get kind of loud at night sometimes, though." Jamey looked at me and wiggled his eyebrows, a teasing look in his eyes. Even knowing he was teasing, I couldn't help my blush.

Dante set down the pans he was carrying, then turned to walk back out of the kitchen past Jamey. At Jamey's comment about us being loud, Dante smacked him on the back of his head as he passed.

"Don't embarrass my girl," Dante said mildly.

"But it's fun," Jamey yelled at Dante's back as he continued on out of the apartment, propping the door open behind him. Jamey walked over to me, put his arm around my shoulders and gave them a quick squeeze.

"You know I'm just teasing you, honey, right?" He looked down at me with a smile.

I put my arm around his waist and returned the hug.

"Of course I do. You love to make me blush. Dante's just a little overprotective."

"Am not," we heard from outside where Dante could obviously hear our conversation.

Jamey and I looked at each other and said at the same time, "Yeah, right." Laughing, we broke apart and got to setting up the food.

People started to arrive soon after that. Cal and Kendrick arrived first. I'd spent much less time with Cal than with Kendrick and Jamey since he was out of town so much, so I was glad to have a chance to talk with him before everyone else arrived. Cal was gorgeous – dark hair, smokey gray eyes, and a barely-there scruff that was sexy as hell. He was talkative, charming, and had a smile that could stop you in your tracks. He was so different than Kendrick that it was hard to believe they were twins. Kendrick was equally attractive, but he was a quiet observer who didn't call attention to himself. Oddly enough, although Cal was the more outgoing of the two by far, it felt to me like he would be the harder one to really get to know. He seemed like an open book on the surface, but I wasn't so sure that was all there was to Callahan Reid.

Dev arrived next and then Meg a little bit later. Dev had become somewhat of a regular at the pub and he dove right into conversation with the guys. I was surprised to see that Meg was alone since she had said that Aaron would be coming with her. She said that he was working, then quickly changed topics, making it clear that she didn't want to talk about it, at least right then. I was debating whether to poke at it gently or just drop it when my attention was caught by Jamey walking out of my propped open apartment door. What grabbed me was his reaction when he noticed that Meg had arrived. He hesitated for just a second and there was a quick flare of interest in his eyes. It was more than just a man casually noticing an attractive woman, which of course Meg was. It was intense and focused. Then Jamey dropped his eyes, and when he looked up, it was like it hadn't happened at all. It was very interesting and definitely something I'd be keeping an eye on during the party.

We had a great time hanging out, eating, drinking and enjoying a beautiful afternoon. Callahan was telling us a hilarious story about the tour that the band he managed had just finished, when I noticed a woman walk slowly up the steps and stand quietly at the top. No one seemed to notice her at first, or at least I thought they hadn't. I looked over at Dante, and the huge grin on his face told me that not only had he seen her, but he knew her and was very happy she was there.

Just then, Jamey spoke up, interrupting Cal's story.

"Well, I'll be damned. If it isn't Princess Ellie."

All eyes turned toward the woman who now had a huge smile on her face. As Jamey rose to go to her, I looked over at Dante. He nodded, confirming that the woman was his younger sister, Elena, known as Ellie.

"Surprise, everybody!" Ellie held her arms out and as Jamey reached her, he swept her off her feet, spinning her in a circle, both of them laughing like kids. Watching them, my gaze wandered over the others, then stopped when I reached Cal. His posture was still relaxed, but instead of the smile I'd expected, he stared intently at Jamey and Ellie, his jaw clenched. I made a mental note to ask Dante about that later. Jamey set Ellie on her feet, rocked her back and forth in a hard hug, then set her at arm's length, hands still on her shoulders.

"Damn, princess. It's been forever. Where the hell have you been keeping yourself?"

"Here, there, and everywhere." Ellie shook her head and smiled. "I'll tell you the whole long story another day. Right now, I just want to catch up with everybody."

Keeping his arm around Ellie's shoulders, Jamey led her toward our group. "Well, then let's get you a drink and let you get started."

Dante stood up and gave Ellie a hug, then introduced her to me, Dev, and Meg. Apparently, he had known she was coming but kept her secret so she could surprise everyone. With her standing next to Dante, I could see the resemblance I hadn't immediately noticed when she'd appeared at the top of the steps. Same dark eyes, same dark hair, though she had much more of that than Dante, thankfully for her, and same warm tone to her skin. She was beautiful – a slightly younger, much slimmer and shorter version of Dante.

After Dante introduced her to us, he moved aside to give Cal a chance to hug her.

"Good to see you, princess. You're looking beautiful as always." Cal stepped away from Ellie, smile now firmly in place.

"Thanks, Cal. You're being a charmer as always. It's good to see you, too."

Ellie returned Cal's smile, then turned toward Kendrick. He met her eyes, but didn't stand up or make any move in her direction. The smile faded from her face a bit.

"Hi, Kendrick." Ellie sounded a little hesitant, as if she wasn't sure how Kendrick would respond.

Kendrick nodded at her and responded with a single word. "Ellie."

Clearly there was a lot going on here that I didn't understand. Ellie had shown up out of nowhere, Cal had looked intense as he'd watched her and Jamey, and Kendrick didn't seem to be a fan of Ellie's at all. Add that to the heated look Jamey had given Meg earlier and there was a lot going on under the surface of our casual get together. If there was one thing I was learning about this group, it was that things were never uneventful for long.

As if he'd heard my thoughts from his seat next to me, Dante turned to me with his gorgeous smile lighting up his face. He reached for my hand, twining our fingers together.

"You sure you want to sign up for this?" He nodded toward the group now laughing and chatting again near us.

"I do." As I heard my response, it sounded like a promise of things to come. Seeing Dante's eyes darken, I knew he heard it, as well. "I want it all."

Dante raised my hand to his lips and kissed it.

"It's yours then, baby. All of this" - he nodded again toward the group with another grin - "God help you, and, I promise you, all of me."

The End

Ready for more from the Brothers Pub world?
Look for Meg and Jamey's story in Believe in Me *(Brothers Pub Book 2)!*

Author bio

Kristyn DeMaster is a contemporary romance author. She writes everyday heroes and heroines who are finding their way to once-in-a-lifetime love through all of life's up and downs. She's a true believer in happily-ever-after and is living hers with her very own romance hero and their fur babies in the American Midwest.

www.ingramcontent.com/pod-product-compliance
Lightning Source LLC
Chambersburg PA
CBHW070029120726
47909CB00003B/1106